ALPI

Head in the Clouds – Book 3

C.E. Wright

Knoxville, Tennessee
crippledbeaglepublishing.com

Cover art created by bobooks, https://www.fiverr.com/bobooks
Manuscript artwork and cover art design created by C.E. Wright

Follow on Twitter @CE_WRIGHT8

Paperback ISBN 978-1-958533-48-2, 978-1-958533-49-9
Hardcover ISBN 978-1-958533-47-5, 978-1-958533-50-5

Library of Congress Control Number: 2023919636

Printed in the United States of America

Praise for *Petrichor,*
Book 1 of the *Head in the Clouds* Series

"Wright is an eloquent writer whose imagery makes you feel like you are soaring in the skies of Petrichor with Hurricane, wind kissing your feathered body. [...] I really enjoyed reading the dynamics of Hurricane's relationships between family and friends, [which] translate to real life and can be quite relatable. I'm curious to see how these relationships will play out as the plot develops and what other characters may enter the picture."
—Clara H.

"Overall, a really enjoyable and quick read, and I think about the characters pretty frequently in my day.
Also, a dragon book without humans? Win!"
—Daniel A., professional animator

"I think Hurricane is a great character and has a lot of depth [...] Windshift is a great character, and when Hurricane meets him is probably my favorite scene of the book[...]
All in all, very great story and I kept wanting to read to see what happened."
—Matthew L.

"I'm excited to see more from this series! Would recommend to Wyvern and Dragon lovers, a new great fantasy series is taking flight!"
—User "cooooooool" on Amazon

"Petrichor is beautifully written. I went into it with high hopes and was not disappointed. It made me laugh, contemplate, and gave me one or two shocks. Altogether a pleasant reading experience and I look forward to more from Wright soon."
—Margaret S.

"I would not have expected such a short book to give so much[...] The social abuse by members [of] the dominant priest caste, and a backstory forcing the [main character] Hurricane to earn her family's keep, are cause for many hardships she overcomes as she can, doing what she must, unfaltering. And the progressive exposition delivers some good, unexpected slaps and surprises."
—Pierre K.

"I read this in one sitting on the day of my birthday. What a treat it turned out to be! I love reading about dragons who can't bear to kill sheep. The setting is fascinating, too. There's lots of magic in it that separates it from the everyday, but at the same time a flawed society is depicted by an author who knows they are depicting plausible flaws."
—Ryan N.

"I bought this book for my sister and she absolutely loved it. I have never seen her read a book so fast. She brought it with her everywhere. If you or someone you know is into well written fantasy books, then this is perfect. It also inspired her to start writing which is just amazing. 10/10. I would definitely recommend."
—Gabrielle G.

Praise for *Kalder,*
Book 2 of the *Head in the Clouds* Series

"I loved book 1, but I think I love this one even more. It was so descriptive and exciting. I really feel like I'm getting to know Hurri's character even more... and I'm sensing a romance brewing between her and Sparik. Can't wait to see where they go next!"

—Gayle W.

"As the first one, this book carries a lot more than would be expected for such a short read. The immersion in Hurricane's mind is efficient in its simplicity, as she starts the quest she's been entrusted with, and things seem not as simple as she wished. It differs from the first book though, in that half of the former was introducing her life and struggles in a very unusual way; leaving the reader to connect the dots. This one is more turned to the action, the character being introduced."

—Pierre K.

"Kalder is extremely well written. Building on themes established in the first book, it plays a lot with point of view, and the character development is really interesting. It also handles languages in a unique and dynamic way. I am immensely intrigued to find out what happens next, so this series has sufficiently hooked me. Totally worth the read."

—Ansley

To every teacher and every professor who helped me develop
my craft.

Sincerely,
Chloe

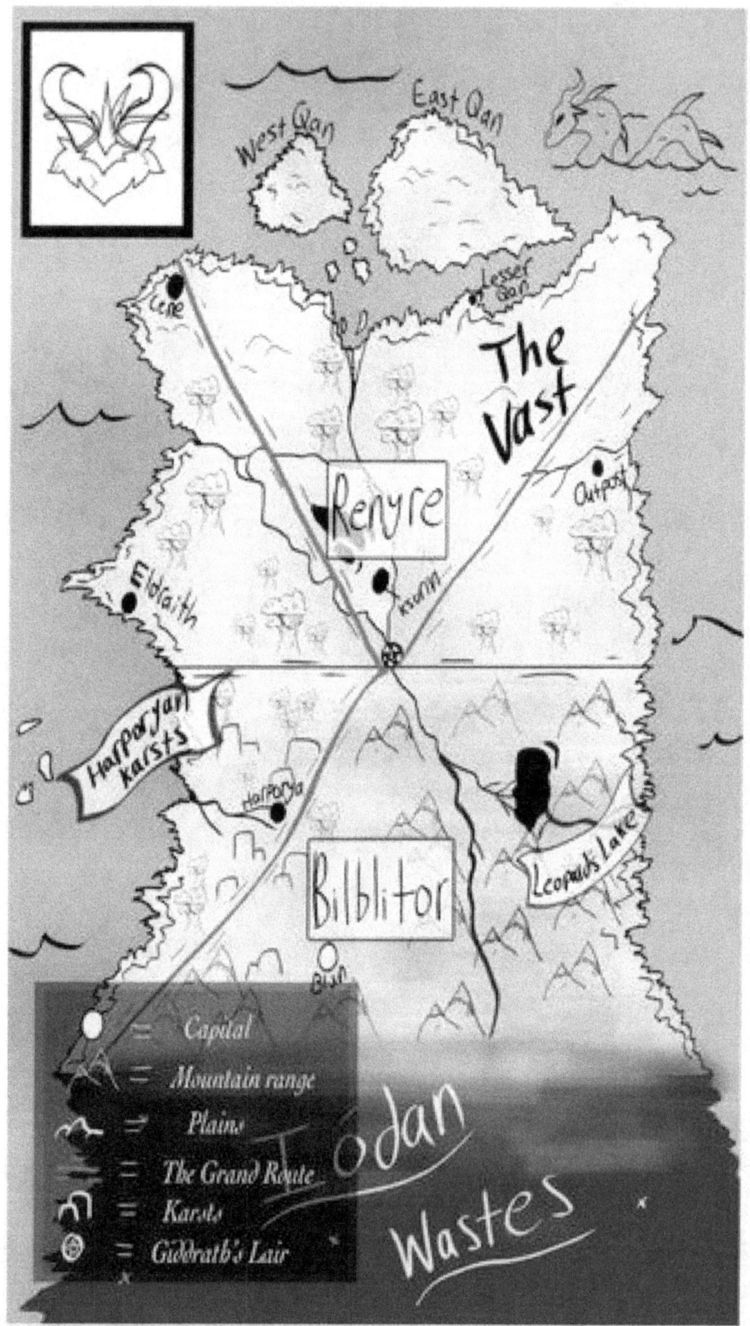

West Qan
East Qan
Lesser Qan
The Vast
Cire
Renyre
Outpost
Ksann
El'diraith
Harporjan karsts
Harporja
Bilblitor
Leopards Lake
Qian
Capital
Mountain range
Plains
The Grand Route
Karsts
Giddrath's Lair
Todan
Wastes

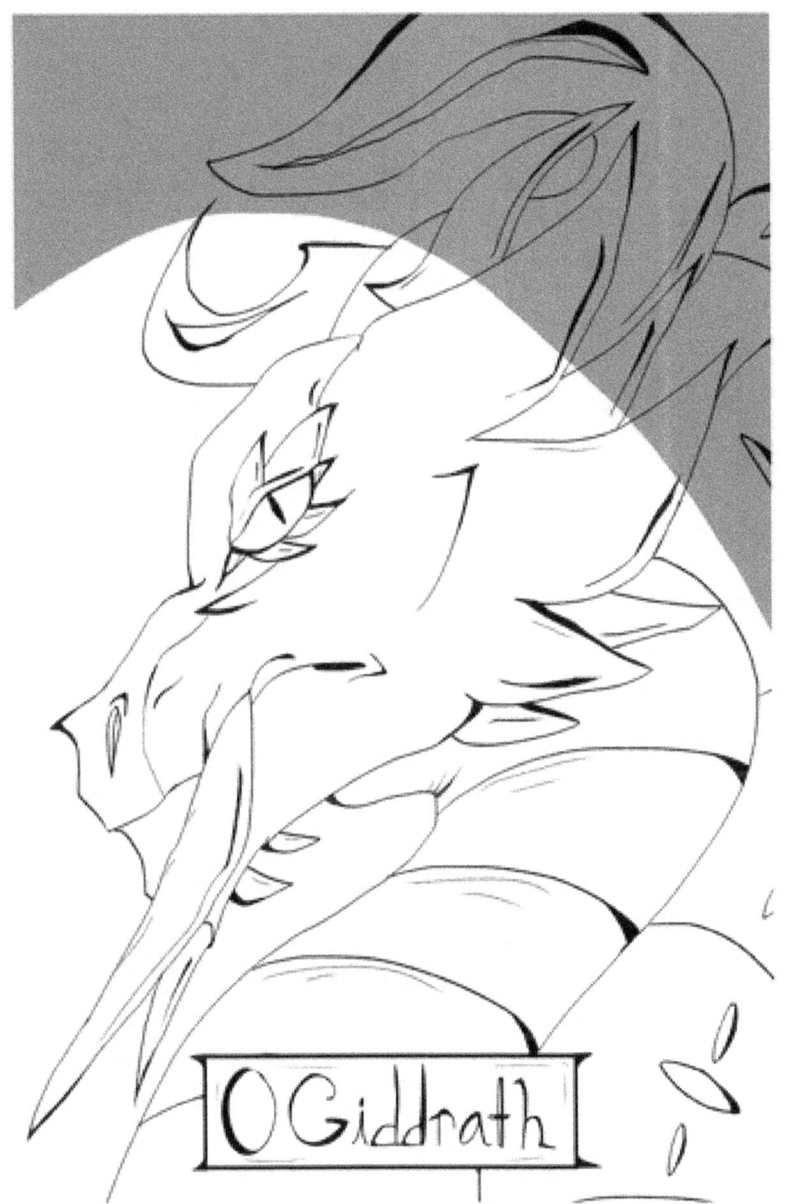
Giddrath

'I exist.' In thousands of agonies — I exist!
Fyodor Dostoyevsky

Chapter I

HURRICANE

I can't count the number of times I've stared into the hollow eyes of death. My talons are tired, and I am hungry.

Now, those talons are grabbing palm fronds and balancing them on my back. I hop across the streams of the turquoise tide pools and consider rushing back to my basecamp to fetch my basket. I have artfully woven some leaves into a bowl to gather the remaining rainwater dripping from the trees. I have crossed my own streams, but who is to support me? My wings. They carried me to this island. From here, I can make it through everything. I'm not invincible, but I've seen enough for me to understand the world of Onverra (I hope).

I look at my bounty. Judging by the fronds, unripe coconuts, and bark yanked from the palm trees, I think I have enough. Now I need to make it back to my home away from home.

The territory is easily traversable, and the sand is as familiar. I've known it for two days now. If someone takes the talon prints I've made, lays them out in a line, and circles them around the island, they will wrap around three or four times. But I cannot back up my logic; I flunked math.

I arrive at the hut. Honestly, I'm proud of the roof here. I could've used my own wings, but I didn't want to hold them up for too long. Here goes the bark, and in this little hole I dug goes the coconuts. These fronds need to be put on top. Or I could fashion them into a door. Who knows?

As I walk through the deeper parts of the little house, I am more and more impressed with myself. One wyvern made this whole little shelter happen. Okay, here it is dry, and if I move the roof like this, a little light can shine in. I can close it like that. And firmly too. Waves and waves of storms have been passing through, and while I miss the taste of rainwater and wind, Sparik won't.

Watching his wrapped body stops the flow of my pride instantly. I made all of this happen. Sure, I constructed the hut. He has not stirred since he saw the eyes of his father.

I put my talon on his chest. At least I hear thudding, wherever his heart is. *Of course he has a heart.* He saved me, so of course I saved him in return. It is only right. I only hope that if– when he wakes up, he will continue to be my guide.

What seems to be a cough leaves his body. The cough is more of a hacking, but the noise is enough for me to jolt and hold his face in my talons. I analyze every twitch of his scales. Anything for him to come back and help me on my quest.

His eyes struggle to open. He squints and glances back and forth as if trying to understand his surroundings. He sees me. "Hurr… H-Hurricane?"

"Sparik, you're back."

He touches the vine rug I had also meticulously woven (doesn't mean it was *well* woven) and clenches the leaves. "*W-where am I?*"

"Here, rest."

He tries to sit up from his resting place and winces harshly at his knees. Grabbing them tightly, he looks for an answer from me.

I give one. "I couldn't take us back to Kalder. The kingdom has an order on our heads if we touch Kalder's soil. We can continue into Alpi safely."

He freezes.

"Do you remember that?"

Something convulses in his face. "Yes. Yes, I suppose I do."

"We're on an island in the ocean. About an hour flight to …" I fish for the book and find the map for Alpi. I turn to show him the pages and see he has fallen back asleep, and his snoring rustles the paper.

The new, mountainous land stretches farther than Petrichor and Kalder combined. The land is rich in woodland, rivers, and rock. The Giddrathians can rip out the roots from all of that nature in an instant. While I wait for him to wake again, I walk outside the hut. I may be small, but I can be fiercer than them, and anyone or anything else on this island that might attack us.

If Windshift's sketches didn't accurately represent life in Kalder, that must mean Alpi is no different. I slow my pace and try to stomach the nerves. *So, who knows what truly lies in those forests?*

Sparik coughs, at last, and I rush back inside.

"Are you feeling better?" I ask.

"At … at least I can talk."

"Do you want anything to drink?"

"Quick, grab my canteen. From my satchel."

I follow orders and nudge the bottle to him. He grunts as he props himself up with his arm, but when that fails, I stretch my wing under his back to hold him up.

"Try to take sips. How long do we need to make this lava last?"

"Until we land on Alpi and find some mud. I can harness some light magic and boil out the impurities. Not the most pleasant taste, but it'll have to do. Damned sun," he says, capping the bottle, "I should've planned better."

I will tolerate no self-deprecating talk today. "Hey. We survived." *Somehow.*

"How?" he asks himself. When his eyes take in the inside of the hut, every hour put into the waterproof ceiling, every minute put into the food storage area, he chuckles.

"What's so funny?"

"I had the most bizarre revelation. You saved me." He gazes at me in wonder. "The last moment I remember is losing consciousness over the open sea, the waves raging underneath … Did you–"

"Seconds before you hit the water, I swooped down and grabbed you."

"You carried me? Me?"

"With difficulty and a strong dose of adrenaline. I found some other deserted islands that spotted the ocean, and we rested for a bit. I really, really didn't know I could carry something your size or weight." I look at my legs. My talons must have fantastic muscles by now. "The craziest thought for me is how none of this seems possible without Windshift. I don't know if his magic can possibly move through the portal, but in my soul, I couldn't have done that alone. He helped in some way. I know it."

He stares silently. "Incredible."

"Isn't it?"

Chapter II

I shudder at the mouse bones piled in the corner. He tried to eat the critter quietly in order not to turn my stomach. I snack on nuts and berries instead.

After some contemplative resting, I think about our next steps. "Did you pack any cloaks or robes for disguises?" He nods and gestures at his bag again. At the sight of two cloaks for each of us, I remember my homemade backups. "Say, I have more disguises planned out. I found these sharp leaves from a pineapple, plastered them together with some wet clay, and made tusks." I nose around a burrow underneath the wall and toss them at Sparik's feet. "What do you think?"

He picks one up and investigates its crevices. He laughs again, the color in his scales finally returning.

"What now? Is my craftsmanship not suitable enough for you?"

"No. No, it's not that." He angles the point of the vibrant green tooth at me. "You have made yourself quite the weapon. But the tusks are not of this color."

"Right. Of course. I can find some more clay to make it more realistic."

"By the way, how long was I out?"

"Two days or so."

"Two days? Honestly?" His talons go to his face as his eyes widen. "What are we doing here? By Kaozar's fire–" He sighs, bites the inside of his cheek, and grabs his bag.

"I'll bring what I can from the hut." While I collect my satchel and any spare food I've attempted to dry, I ask, "How do we get to Giddrath's castle without raising suspicion?"

"That's an excellent question. I don't feel well enough to answer right now. May I ask one small favor?"

I nod.

"Will you help me outside?"

I take his talon and lead him to the entrance of the hut. We duck our heads and touch the sunbaked sand. "Why do you need to go outside to answer a question?"

Sparik changes. His talons twitch at the sunbeams shooting down. A glow cascades down his scales, and his fire grows slowly but surely brighter. He rolls his neck, straightens his body, and lets out a long-repressed sigh. He turns back to me. I've never seen such a relieved smile. *Or a quicker recovery.* My own smile grows. The sun gracing my cheeks makes them warmer than ever. *Well, I couldn't be blushing, could I?* His words shake me out of my daze. "We must enter through the northern harbors. I'd suggest Eldraith. Do you know where that is?" I nod. *Yes, it must've been only the sun.* "Good. We can slip in without seeming too out of place because of the diversity of those ports and find our way south."

"Are you sure you can fly?"

Stretching out his arms, he skips on the sand. "Oh, what marvelous weather this is."

I gape at his youthful body frolicking around the beach as if nothing in the past few days happened. "It sure is."

After packing up and saying a tearful goodbye to my magnificent architectural achievement, we set flight. I start before Sparik and am pleasantly surprised at him twisting and turning in the air. The light hugs the wrinkles in his tattered shirt.

His laughs ring through the air. "I need no one to carry me. Not a soul."

We fly silently for a while, and Sparik is still smiling. *What is going through his head? I hate to say it; his smile is a tad annoying. He's happy. Why should I be annoyed? He has been freed from the responsibility of the role of the Advisor and from his corrupt family. Perhaps that's what's vexing him in the first place. This is a huge upheaval in his life. His father practically disowned him. His god disowned him. I need him in a genuinely positive mood for this quest to come to fruition. We need to talk about this.*

"Sparik?

"What?"

"I can only imagine how you're feeling. I know you must be really hurting right now. Your brother and father have horribly mistreated you and exiled you from your own kingdom. Your mother didn't even stand by your side. If you want to talk, I'm–"

"Hey, Hurricane, I have so many questions to ask you." He dips in and out of the clouds. "What do you even do? What's your direction in life? We never got to talk about that."

"We did not." *For good reason. If he is to be my ally, I have to let some walls down. I stayed in that cell for two weeks waiting for him, and he did come around. I'll tell him something.* "I'm a student."

"A student. Studying what?"

He really wants me to entertain him. If my words distract him long enough, he won't lose his head. "Biology."

"Biology." He flips around in the sky. "Do you aim to become a scientist?"

"Not sure. A job there would pay for my parents and brother's house. It's hard to get a job there anyway when you're like me."

"What do you mean?"

I stick my head through the clouds and notice the new shade of light blue in the sky. New hues are everywhere. "My mother has to take care of my father all the time." *Can I even mention the word* Father *around him without him potentially spiraling?*

"What's wrong with your father?"

"He's been sick for two years. We *all* have to take care of each other in that dingy neighborhood. There are about a dozen dingy neighborhoods all along the swamp border that go through the same thing as we do."

"That sounds awful."

As if he would know. Be nice, Hurricane. "A part of me feels as if we don't deserve it. Out of everyone, we should be exempt from this bizarre system that plagues our kingdom. I work days and nights. I pay my dues. Since Windshift put me on this quest, I feel special again." My reflection in the ocean water glares back. "When I am able to set aside some money for myself, do you wanna know what I'd want?"

He perks up. "What?"

"Corn. For my sheep, mainly. I tried some, and I totally understand the appeal. Usually, I only see higher class citizens purchasing some. They can afford it way more than I can, hah. When I get my talons on it, all my hard work is worth it. Baa will live a happier life than I can, under my wing."

"Your work must be incredibly strenuous– Wait, wait, wait. Is the sheep's name Baa?"

Thankful that he changed the subject mid-sentence, I say, "Yes."

He cackles, his smile spreading farther. The sound is airy and high-pitched, and it startles a bird half a league away. "Why'd you name him after the sound he makes?"

"Because … Because … I'd thought it'd be cute."

He cackles even harder, letting the laughter pour out like a wound untended to. "Well, what about your job?"

That right there is something I'm not telling him as long as I can manage it.

"I …"

He tilts his head in confusion. He spies the distance and beams. "There! Right there. See?"

At least he's attentive and merry. "Where?"

The spine of a mountain range appears, mist clouds hanging over the peaks. Before it is dense deciduous forest. In front of the greenery is the harbor. Alpi is a monolith.

Chapter III

My stress is at the same level as it was when I arrived at Kalder, but the feeling is different. I had nothing except my book and Windshift's wishes on that sweltering continent; here, the contact with the soft breeze tossing my fur around and Sparik's rambling put me at ease. However, these dragons are different from the Kaozari. My worst fear is realized when seeing the first Giddrathian on two legs hauling a barrel from a boat; the Giddrathians are much, much larger.

The brown dragon picks up and places the sloshing barrel on the back of a fellow Giddrathian's cart. The rider, an orange dragon, summons a beast to grumble awake and move forward, pulling the cart. What I can catch from my obscured vision (the population is as teeming as Eilora) is the brown and black striped fur of the flat-nosed creature. I turn to Sparik. "Are you seeing this?"

"I see it every day. Let's land on that pier."

By this point, we have pulled off our appearance flawlessly. With the help of my newly born socio-political knowledge, I deduced that we must not appear as Giddrathians but rather their allies the Surrvesians to properly disguise ourselves, so to wear the pineapple leaf tusks would seem like a tacky costume. Surrvesians have large horns and light scales. We needed to cover up our nose horns and paste Sparik's scales with a sand-mud mixture. He suggested wearing masks back at the hut. Since we're in the northern harbors, our masks would easily protect us from the wind gusts, so we would seem practical and well-prepared. All was going according to plan until I needed to learn how to stand on two legs.

I float down and remember my training. Sparik said, and I don't know if it was an insult, "I have never had a student this insolent before to not know how to stand on two legs." Other than the occasional griffin and Kaozari on the Alvoreçeri islands, no one walks using their wings as I do. Sparik insisted I know how to walk bipedally, especially when we travel to the Surrvesian lands.

"You're doing great," Sparik whispers. I glance down and gasp as quietly as I can. I didn't even notice that I was already walking on the matted dirt ground. I was distracted, ranting to myself about the walking itself. While I look around, the Giddrathians don't even bat an eye. Their baggy fur coats billow behind their warm-toned scales as they go from cart to cart and stall to stall. I wrap the cloak tightly around my scales. The wind is not my friend today.

A professional-looking sign hangs over a booth where the tusked dragons bow and speak to a creature I have never seen before. No scales surround its face or body. In fact, the short creature is fleshy. I believe what encompasses it is called skin. The skin covering the hands is paler than the rest, the color of a pine tree. The russet fur on the creature's head is pulled back to show prominent cheekbones.

"What species is that?" I ask Sparik, nudging him.

"She's a dwarf," he says, trying to stop his teeth from chattering. "I'm going to ask her directions to the nearest tavern."

My guide walks over to the dwarf and bows to her. Now, I hear a new language. "*Tanwen, eidral ylldrid?*"

Her dark eyes light up. *"Aye, vadsuye. Peloh, ghrek fuaein?"* She points to the two of us. I straighten my posture, and with a side eye from Sparik, I bow as well.

The dwarf returns to her customers, and Sparik tells me to follow him. We will stay at the bar for a brief respite to get our bearings. "Believe me, I haven't eaten anything more than a mouse for too long."

"We had those dried fruits in my bag."

He flattens his mouth and gives me a look. *He's so picky.* I scoff and follow him down the dirt pathway, each grain trampled by large, clawed dragon footprints.

The wind picks up, and I understand the *northern* part of the northern harbor. Only an hour away is the temperature humid and cumbersome. The market is at least two leagues higher in elevation. I wrap the mask closer to my face and do what I would call halfway hyperventilating. As long as I hyperventilate enough, that sign in the distance will appear even closer. The Giddrathians don't even bother with the icy gale and instead are bantering with each other. From the belly of one of them, a laugh pierces through the hubbub of the market. More start to arise. Something in my veins strips away at my guard.

Sparik and I arrive at the tavern, a two-story log building amidst towering, deciduous trees. We nod to the dwarves sitting and fidgeting with pipes on the patio. Their smoke becomes thicker as we enter the fragrant and crowded interior. Patrons come and go. "You know the drill," Sparik says. "Follow my lead."

If I was walking on four legs right now, my head would reach the top of the circular tables where the dragons sit. They shift in their seats and eye us and our darkly colored clothes. By Windshift's mighty lightning, these creatures have extremely wide shoulders!

I plop down on the wooden stools at the dimly lit bar with Sparik, who leans over the counter. He murmurs something to the bartender and circles an item on a sheet of paper. The tavern master responds with a grunt. She peers down at me and nods.

"Circle what you'd like," Sparik says, pointing to the paper in front of him. I peer at a list of items and whisper to Sparik for a vegetarian option. In a land of strong dragons such as these, I'm sure they've eaten meat all their life. Sparik proves me wrong by showing me a list of dishes decorated with filigree. I point to one of them and wait. Mother told me to eat my vegetables when we had them, so I hope that she will be honored by this.

Acoustic music plays from a radio. It is the one small item or entity in this room, and I find myself surprised. *I thought radios were exclusively created by wyverns. The only one I've seen was at university and significantly larger, probably to relay information to a larger group.* At least the music is calming and at the perfect decibel for me to hear my conversation with Sparik.

"I ordered that one," he says, gesturing to the dwarf behind us. I struggle to hold in my laughter.

The small, fleshy creature's dragon friend widens his mouth and inhales runny potatoes, fried turkey legs, and *corn. Delicious.* He slurps them up and sighs, satisfied. The dwarf shakes his head, takes the plate from the Giddrathian, and inhales the food even deeper. They look at each other and laugh uproariously. I bet that small creature can't even hold up the plate, but I mustn't underestimate living beings I've never heard of before now.

"I believe I got that and a side of peach stew. Ahhh, I love peaches."

He stares in the distance and touches on each benefit of eating a peach until our meals come. I let him talk since that might be what he needs right now, a distraction in the form of juicy fruits.

Our food and drink arrive. I might as well start eating Giddrathian food now, so I won't be picky during our treks. This mushroom steak overwhelms me with a suspicious odor. I sniff it again and can't wrap my head around what is so wrong with the mushroom. I nibble on one of the fried potato pancakes on the side that dips its edges in the pool of suspicious sauce.

"Why'd you order that?" I ask, gesturing to his granite mug.

"Everyone drinks at a bar." He brings the cup to his mouth and makes a polite slurping noise. Then he shows me the cup, the liquid inside the same level as it was before.

"Hah. Wow. How inconspicuous."

"Please cover for me. You can drink yours, and we can switch mugs to make it seem as if I finished."

I drink my water in three gulps. "Well, what did you order?"

"Basic, tavern brewed mead." I make a face. "If you don't want to drink that, don't worry–"

"Shh. I'm not a coward." I grab the mug and yank it to my mouth. First impressions? I have definitely tasted worse. The smell is all too familiar. I glance back at my mushroom steak. "Is it common for Giddrathian cuisine to put alcohol in their food?"

"Common? Basically every day."

The most we wyverns do is cook wine into our sauces. Do even the little broodlings drink mead as soon as they hatch? This may be an acquired taste, but I don't have to get used to it. I sip until the cup is halfway full. I make another face.

Sparik notices my scrunched-up nose, and worry appears in his expression again. I won't let another outburst happen. "Nothing's wrong. The smell is unfamiliar, yes, but everything else is fine. I already feel stronger."

"Hm, if you say so." He devours his turkey legs. I flick off a piece of meat flown at me from his ravenousness.

After a smooth horn solo is about to close out a song, a jingle plays from the radio.

Sparik translates without moving his mouth, "Global breaking news. I- I don't know what it's about– Wait, I know that voice." I finish my last bite as the speech abruptly transitions to a new voice, the one I wanted to hear the least. My handkerchief plummets to the counter.

"Dragons and domained creatures of Onverra, a mighty peril is amongst our kind. Not only does it affect me, but it affects each and every one of you. Someone who our kingdom trusted– someone *I* trusted– has betrayed us and escaped to pursue dark magic and resurrect terrible evils. You may know him as well as I did … or as well as I thought I did. I as the new Advisor of Kalder demand, with the permission of O Giddrath's Advisor–"

The radio static chops up his sentences, and the bartender fiddles with the dial until Faolani's voice returns.

"The death of Sparik, ex-prince and son of Kaozar, and his female accomplice Perra Hurri–" The static eats his words– "banished from our continent. My council and I have reason to believe that he is hiding out somewhere in Alpi–" I hear more unintelligible garble. "My coronation…they disgraced my visage…and they'll disgrace yours without a quiver in their hearts unless we stop them."

The civilians in the tavern scratch their claws against the wooden tables. A discussion begins, and I am left in the dust as it continues. What I can do is let the new information sink in. *What changed between our departure and now? Why does he want us dead? Why did another official even approve of this nonsense? They don't even know me. If this announcement is global ... could that mean my family heard? Is that possible? Thank Windshift that the radio signal was incompetent. I cannot let anyone know my name.*

Sparik grips his knife and bores his eyes into my soul. He softly shakes his head, and it's a miracle I even noticed he did.

"What are they saying?" I hope he can read mouths.

He leans over and flips through the menu and points to random items. As he does, he answers. "The group in the corner there thinks they should follow orders from Varsunynth and be vigilant. That family across the room doesn't think they should follow Faolani's demands, even if their own Advisor approves of them." He pulls his cloak tighter at the exposure of the dark red scales of his feet. The sand-mud mixture obscures less than we thought. "A chance stands that they won't attack since they don't want to follow a Kaozari's orders, but since *somehow* Varsunynth wanted this, they'll jump at the chance to kill me. They hate me." He leans back over his meal, and I catch him saying, "Everyone hates me."

I catch a look at the dragons discussing what to do. I feel as if I'm not even here. They're speaking about us as if we weren't, and I had best not make any move to make it seem as if we are. "We have to get out of here now and hide."

"I know," Sparik says. "But how?"

"We're isolated from them. Isn't that kind of suspicious? We should act as if we're part of the conversation and slip out."

"That exit back there," he says, flicking his tail under the cape toward the side door as someone reeking of leftover meat and wearing an apron walks in, "might work, since the chefs are taking out the trash. We can slip out as they come in. Let's turn and calmly take a couple of steps. I leave first, and you leave half a minute later. Keep your mask tight. I've disguised myself plenty of times, but I've never been a fugitive before now." *Me neither!*

I nod at the speech given by one Giddrathian, who climbs on a table and holds up a pamphlet. The paper depicts Faolani in black robes, but he's not how I've seen him before we escaped. *The scar spread even farther across his face, like wildfire. His left eye is completely gone, and his jaw might be next. The left horn looks as if a shark took a bite out of a branch of dying coral. Faolani doesn't hide any inch of the carnage. He wants the world to know what we did.*

I can imagine what the speech giver must be saying. "For he is a beast, but if our own ilk sides with him…" He lowers the paper and sighs. "I can barely believe I'm siding with a Kaozari. We must kill them on sight. We can appease our goddess."

He does the one thing, the one immeasurable thing, I didn't want him to do.

He looks at me.

"*T'wen, sosdk jonta?*"

"He just asked for your opinion," Sparik whispers. He thinks for a second.

The dragon is impatient. "*Zol?*"

"Repeat after me. *Ghrek Varsunynth sholn, vad sholn.* It means 'Wherever our Advisor goes, I go.'" *Are you crazy? You're calling for our death.*

I proclaim, "*Gnek Varsunhynth sholn, vad sholn.*"

The tavern goes silent. They nod at each other in what I hope is agreement.

"You had a Bilblitorian accent when you spoke, and this is a local bar. Also," he says, gulping, "you pronounced ghrek wrong. Everyone pronounces that in the same way."

"*Parne ot Bilblitor? Eidsuye manent long,*" the dragon says.

"I understood 'long.'"

"You're– we're here on business. Repeat after me." I do, and the Giddrathian tilts his head in interest.

Once our conversation ends, the dragon bows and returns to his bar mates. He gives us a warm welcome, but we won't overstay it.

"Now I'll leave," Sparik says. He hops off the stool and walks through the side door but not before snagging a bread roll from his plate. I count in my head for thirty seconds then follow after him. My tail bumps into an unoccupied chair, which harshly scrapes on the floor. I bend down, put the chair in its original position, and continue. It feels so good to be back on my four legs again. *Wait a second.*

Someone clears their throat behind me. I whip around and see the bartender. She gestures at my legs, and I come back up immediately. A confused Sparik pops his head out from the door and notices the predicament. He bows and hopefully explains why I walked on four legs. I nod frantically in agreement, even though I have no idea what he's saying.

The bartender targets him next and gasps at his exposed feet. Sparik's shoulders rise as he backs up into the door.

I start following him, but at the feeling of motion above my head, I freeze. My interrogator has my cloak in her talons and stares at me as if I have five heads. Without a second of hesitation, she leaps to Sparik and yanks off his hood.

We meet each other's eyes. The cloaks are dropped on the floor.

The dragons and dwarves step away from their chairs and wield what weapons they have. The flesh creatures have daggers, but the Giddrathians have their own talons, which is far more intimidating. One of them has her palms glimmering with green magic. She rubs a leaf in between her claws, and with a whoosh, I duck and gaze up at a vine that sunk its thorns into the door behind me. The dragon jerks the vine back, taking a chunk of the wood with her. I jump, snatch both cloaks, and slip through the door, Sparik following suit.

The tavern goers chase us as we run down the alley, which stinks with the smell of dead fish. Sparik turns and snaps his fingers toward the ground. An aggressive fire blocks the path and towers over the crowd. "Where in the world should we hide?" I ask.

"Um, uh, far from here. Far, far from here. In the woods. We have much less of a target on our backs if we stay in the woods." Sparik skids past a stable, and he trots back at the sight of motion behind the bars. A yellow eye peeps behind the wall and inspects both of us. "Perfect."

"Perfect? What even is that creature?"

He opens the stable door, closes it behind us, and holds out his hand instantly. A monster with shaggy brown fur and large, stocky legs scratches its broad muzzle and stumbles before us. I raise my head to meet its stare and almost squeal. Sparik waits for the creature to come to him, and after plenty of hesitation, the creature sniffs his hand.

"This is an Umerz. They're friendly, this one especially, but only if you're friendly first. Be sure to pet it. We'll ride this one out of here."

"Why can't we fly?" I ask, throwing my cloak back on and tossing the other to him.

"It's too late. They'll be searching for us in the sky." I size up the beast and lift my wing out to it. The beast licks the feathers, and I giggle to cover up the intense albeit endeared disgust.

Sparik hops on the Umerz's back and so do I. *This is at least the third time he's put me in danger like this. But we're still alive.* I debate whether or not I should grab onto his waist, but I have no choice. The beast rustles and slams through the door, knocking me forward into Sparik's back. I hold on for dear life as the beast snarls at the dragons trapped by the fire and carries us into the day.

Chapter IV

We're far, far from the town now. The shadows of the leaves cast down on the thick patches of grass around the path that we bolt down. It's about time we stop, but Sparik has a twitch in his eyes. I haven't let go of his waist, so I notice his shivering along with his body temperature slowly falling as we race up the side of a hill. *How do I get him to rein the Umerz in?*

"Hey, Sparik, we're good," I say. "We can stop now. The dragons are at least an hour away."

"No, no we're not. We'll be fine, we just have to keep going." Sparik says as if trying to string the words together. The beast's paws thud on the dirt, the sound filling Sparik's silence.

In the meantime, the trees stretch across the barely visible sky, the sun peeping through the canopy at least a league above us. Vines twist around the branches and trunks. There is some room for flight but it cannot be compared to Kalder and Petrichor. Perhaps the dragons of this world think that their wings shouldn't be used every day … even though their wings are covered in spikes and are carried cumbersomely on their backs around the marketplace.

"Hold, hold!" Sparik yelps as he yanks the reins of the Umerz.

"Oh no, what's wrong? What happened?"

"We can't cross the river."

As we skid to a stop, I slam into the back of Sparik, who is frozen. I hop down and wonder what is the matter. What greets me is a reasonably narrow river, its water babbling with the chirping of songbirds. *What's going on?*

Sparik ties up the beast to a tree, and he grabs and tosses some dried meat from his bag to it. The Umerz's jaws clamp over the well-earned snack as it rests its furry head on its much furrier paws.

He paces through the grass and stares at the rapids, the sky, and then me. His face plummets, and he sits on the riverbed a sizable distance away from the water. Heaving deep breaths, my guide wrings his talons and stares endlessly into the riverbank. *Does he need space? What should I do? I can comfort   him.*

"Sparik, why don't you want to go through the water? Do you want to talk about it?"

"Well, it's simple. I can't go through the water. Too deep. We can't do it. And that foliage across the water. Too thick. We can't fly through."

"The river is small, at least to me."

"At least to you?"

"Yes. At least to me. You rode well and quickly up that path. If you need a place to rest, then take the time to. The Umerz needs to take a break too. I'll save some water. Is the water good enough to drink here?"

"I don't know," he says, still staring at the currents.

"How come? I thought you knew this place–"

"*I don't know anything.*"

I stop.

"I can't fly. I can't swim. I can't walk. You don't understand. We narrowly escaped that place, and we wouldn't have had to make such a fuss if it wasn't for me. You're in danger again."

"Hey, I started this whole thing by walking on four legs. We agreed to do this together."

"And I stole that Umerz. The owner is probably looking for it, and if whoever it is knew that I was a Kaozari … or knew I was the prince … Everyone already wants me dead. My face is probably on the walls of schools, businesses, castles, even Varsunynth's throne room. I bet tons of daggers are thrown at my scales on those fugitive posters. I can't convince Giddrath or her Advisor to appease us. I can't. Oh, and that ridiculous fire I set to ward off the Giddrathians. I'm an arsonist as well."

"No, *we* are arsonists. I'm your accomplice, right?"

He grasps at his throat. "Of course, of course! I can't forget that my brother wants me dead too. Oh, and my father *also* disowned me in front of my subjects and his creations. My god disowned me." He shakes harder. "I can't do anything. I'm useless. And I'm not going to have us jump over that river, no matter how small it is to you." He buries his head in his hands. "I don't know what to do. My chest hurts, Hurricane. I am cosmically at fault."

While he wraps his arms around his stomach and keels over, my face falls. Back in Petrichor two years ago, Mother, Dust Devil, and I were catching up on some books in the doctor's office. What great trips they were, since we had only read the books at that office and nowhere else. When we didn't want to read everything all at once (if we did, we'd have nothing to do other than wait), we'd look outside. The grass and willow trees flowing in the breeze outside shone brighter in the office's town than in Cirrusmont. I was on page fifty-two of *A Nomad in Tonat* when Dr. Aquamarine told us Father's diagnosis. Mother collapsed at the words: follidotillo disorder. She said her chest hurt too, but she couldn't explain her pain clearly as her breathing was out of control. My ears seemed to blur the noise around when the prognosis was mentioned. My eyesight recognizes each leaf on the trees and as I count them now around me, my head clears.

Even though these burdens of Sparik are heavy on his shoulders and I would have no idea the true details of them, I will help. I will be his guide as he is mine. My walls have cracked. I know his true nature; he is good and everything his brother is not.

"Sparik, describe to me what you see around you."

"W-what do I see?" Tears flood his eyes.

"Look above you. Describe what you see to me."

We gaze at the shimmering filigree of the leaves. "I notice green branches."

"How many?"

"One, two … At least fifteen on the canopy of that tree, and … sixteen on that one."

"Good. Now breathe." He tries. "Do you see any birds?"

He focuses. "I see a dark starling up on that high branch. Looks old." He braces himself and tweets to it. The bird responds and hops from branch to branch.

"What was that?"

"I-it was Giddrathian Hunterspeak."

If this is one of his many areas of knowledge, maybe it'd behoove him to think about it. He needs to know his knowledge. "Tell me about it."

He looks around at the bases of the trees. "Giddrath blessed her dragons with many skills, one of them is mimicking animal noises. They learned to communicate with the birds so they could hunt with them. It's mostly symbiotic; one dragon shares information about a burrow of hedgehogs and the bird about a den of bears."

"What'd you say to the starling?"

"I asked him what he was doing."

"See?" I tap on his arm to get Sparik's attention. "You're anything but worthless. I may look like a bird, but I can never do that."

Sparik sighs and groans, making the starling jolt from his branch. "No, no! It's an archaic language that only the older generation uses. What I taught you isn't even useful. I have zero sense of judgment–"

"That's not true–"

"I can't do anything right. Nothing. Nothing right." He takes a small, metallic tube from his inner pocket and dabs a bit of serum under his tongue.

What I initially believe is the bird tweeting calls my attention. The noise comes from the forest floor, and I never noticed the bird fly down. If anything, Sparik's lamenting must've startled him. I look around to find the source and gasp.

A shriveled creature flops and convulses in the shallow end of the river a minute away. The scales around the long fishtail glitter in the sunbeams, and the whiskers on the creature's face feel around the mud. With horror, I see that where the flesh and the scales meet is a clamp.

"Sparik."

"What?"

This can give him something direct to do. "I need your help."

I urge him each time he hesitates to keep following down the river's edge, then I show him the creature.

He stifles a sob. "What a poor, delicate kit." Sparik reaches to grace the creature's forehead and flinches before he can as the water cascades over its face.

"Kit?"

"This mermaid is only a baby."

"Mermaid?"

"I'll tell you later. Quick, grab my black, stretchy gloves from my bag. You'll know them when you see them." I rush over to the bag and hand him just that. "Thank you." He struggles to slide them on and fixes them firmly around his elbows. "We need to get it out of the water so I can melt the trap open." His eyes dart back and forth between the incoming river flow, the mermaid, and his thin tail. "I can't do it." Sparik gazes hopelessly into the kit's eyes.

Now is the time where I can save him again. "Hold on, Sparik, I got it." I march over to the kit, pull it out of the water, and drag it to the mud. Also, I dab the creature dry with my cloak.

Sparik's face emanates a small glow again. He takes the clamp and glances back and forth from the sunbeams to the now burning metal, twinkling with yellow and rose magic. While the clamp melts, he bends the iron and lets the mermaid feel the freedom of water again. He tosses the clamp into a bush and steps aside. The rush of water greets the mermaid happily. The mermaid chirps at Sparik and I as it floats away, alive as can be.

We return to our bags, and I give him a sip from the lava canteen.

"Do you feel well enough to eat something? I saw you grab that roll."

"Maybe. I'm sorry, I wish I could control my fear of water better. After what happened in front of the volcano and with my brother and father–"

"Sparik, listen to me." We meet each other's gaze. "I will tell you this. You just did a good deed. You didn't have to do it. You could've walked away. Instead, you took action despite everything that's happening. Sure, I helped you, but that showed you can accept help too. We can work together. We're far less than enemies now." I find myself looking deeply into his eyes. "I respect you. Nothing can change that." Sparik gulps and nods. "Do you feel better?"

"I need more time."

"That's alright. Everything will be okay. Now, the Umerz might as well stay with us since it's domesticated, but we will wait for you until you can continue."

Sparik nods, a smile escaping the fear chaining his body down. "We'll still continue our quest. No ridiculous law imposed by my brother can affect our success. We need to knock some sense into Varsunynth the Unassailable first … and by extension, Giddrath." He sits back down, shaking. I put

my talon on his shoulder and wait with him as long as I need
to.

Chapter V

I have good news and bad news. Well, I have one piece of bad news that trumps the several pieces of good news awfully quickly.

Sparik has calmed down since yesterday, after we started along the bank of the river and thankfully found a bridge to cross over. Even though we're a tad off course now, we'll trail down south per the instructions of the map. I trust Sparik's judgment of where Giddrath's lair is, having undoubtedly been there many times as a prince. We have avoided detection from the townspeople, their lantern lights flickering from within the massive, hollowed out redwood tree trunks. Civilians exit their trees and either water their plants, chop wood, or embark on a hunting expedition with a noticeable scarcity of weapons.

As I look upon their homes in the massive tree trunks, I think about the bad news. *We* don't have shelter. We need it too. He and I can't risk camping out even if we had already packed tents. This forest is much more inhabited than Kalder's terrain, so, my building skills don't come in handy here, and we are losing our food stock by the day.

Last night, I thought I heard a hawk and its piercing cry in the distance. Waking from my restless sleep under some brush, I whipped around to spot the creature. Torchlight was dancing in the dark while a pack of Giddrathians marched down the trail. They paused, and the tall, orange dragon in the front cupped her hands and screeched exactly like the bird of prey. The two creatures converse with these cries. I would nudge Sparik to wake up so we could move out, but they were far enough away to where Sparik would have to squint to see them amongst the trees. They wouldn't notice us with our cloaks and the leaf rug I wove back on the deserted island anyway. He stayed warm while snuggling next to the beast and me. In return, I was protected against the night's chills by staying against his scales. As I drift off to sleep, I could only imagine what he was dreaming. *I wish for him to dream of something sweet.* We shouldn't risk being outside. It's better to be packed like sardines instead of at the mercy of the talons of birds of prey.

The Umerz yawns, and Sparik scratches a spot behind its floppy ear. "We need a place to stay the night. I have no idea what to do."

I rub the dark circles under my eyes. *As comfortable as resting around Sparik is, keeping guard of our belongings is more important.* "Me neither. I can't even think of a group that would be willing to let us in anyway. Maybe we can find a place no one is staying in. Do Giddrathians or dwarves often abandon their homes in the trees?"

"Dwarves, more. Giddrathians rarely abandon their trees. Building a house within a tree trunk takes magic, so they feel they shouldn't abandon a place that they helped create. Or a place that is a part of them. Bad news is that dwarf houses …"

"I bet they're tiny."

"They're broodlings' dollhouses to me. They might only be small houses to you. If you were to stay inside and rest, I could stand guard."

"If one of us was to get caught, it definitely shouldn't be you. I can't make it out here alive and convince Giddrath and her Advisor to help us. I don't even speak Giddrathian." *As he well knows,* I think, gulping. Then I have a shattering realization. *He tells me everything. I can't discern culture or customs for myself. Exactly what I didn't want to happen happened; I'm losing my autonomy. I need to save Windshift. I* do. *I feel as foolish as ever for letting Sparik spoon feed me each bit of information I don't know. Sure, I simply don't know anything about this continent, and what I did know in the past is debunked. Still.* My wings feel heavier.

The Umerz grunts and stops suddenly. Sparik pats its head and looks beyond. A sign sticks out of the ground like a bean sprout in front of the beast's paws. Sparik hops down and inspects an area out of my field of vision. He gasps with joy.

"What?"

"You won't believe it. Do you wanna come down?"

I float down and examine the tiny sign. What I can tell is that it's made of wood. That's all. The lettering is blocky at best and uses those little dots on top of As whenever it pleases. Oh, also, I don't speak the language. *The realization I made before we stopped burns even more.*

I sigh. "Can you translate what the sign is saying for me, please?"

He smiles. I feel instantly relieved. "Sure, with pleasure. It's giving information about this refugee home that's taking in Kaozaris."

"Is the sign really that bold to advertise that? Wouldn't that be illegal under Giddrath's law?"

"Well–" *here we go with more spoon feeding–* "everyone on their continent has freedom to do what they want with their god's guidance, as that is one of the gods' gifts. Unfortunately, the Giddrathians take that as a way to harass, abuse, and even murder Kaozaris, whether they want war or not. You see this wood? What do you notice about it?"

The setting sun's last rays shimmer on the freshly polished top of the sign. "Well, the wood is new."

"Yes. The sign was just put up. No one had an opportunity to deface it yet. They could just be starting out business." *Also, we haven't seen a neighborhood in a couple of hours, so there might've been no one to see it at all.* "That might also mean not many refugees are there, so we might be able to show our true scales." He searches through his bag, jots down the address on a small notepad, and mounts the Umerz. "Before sunset, let's ride, get some more provisions, and rest."

The home we arrive at roosts on top of a large oak tree, the branches clawing at the sun. Lights strung on a wire loop around the roof of the house on top of the tree. If this place is not in a tree, maybe it's a dwarf's. *I'm getting better at knowing things on my own ... then again, this needs simple comprehension of context clues and critical thinking. I'm not doing anything special.*

We assist the Umerz at the completely vacant lot (much to Sparik's delight) with lined poles to tie transporting animals on. We walk up the winding stairs and knock on the front door.

A deep voice echoes from inside. "Hm?" Stomping and yawning precede the opening of the door. A dwarf with a fiery orange beard and skin the color of the tree branches adjusts his thin, gold glasses and looks our cloaked selves up and down. Sparik adjusts his mask to show the horn on his nose. The dwarf bows, smiles, and gestures to let us in.

I wait for Sparik to duck his head into the charming, warm living room. The dwarf wipes off excess wood chips from his apron and clasps his hands. Right when I'm feeling comfortable in the orange lighting and inquisitive woodland creatures carved from bark, he speaks Giddrathian. Or Dwarvish. I'm too tired to tell.

Maybe if I can tell what he and Sparik are saying from context clues or body language, I don't have to ask either to translate. Nothing. I can only understand smiles and nods and bows. No "ghreks." No nothing.

Gritting my teeth, I tap Sparik's arm and try to make my tone as pleasant and undemanding as possible. "Will you please ask him if he can speak Kaozari? I would like to understand him."

He takes my request, and I can finally comprehend the dwarf's strong voice. "The name is Scorion. My sister who also runs this safe haven we've built will be here shortly, as she is on a hunting mission." He looks at me. "Will you please remove your mask so I can properly identify you and give you the protection you need?"

Sure, he'll be friendly to Kaozaris. But I'd be profoundly surprised if he was friendly to a wyvern ... since, apparently, they don't know I exist. I look at Sparik's long, forward-facing snout horn, and he gives me the okay to pull down the top of my mask and show my stubby, gray horn on my beak. I do the motion as carefully as he did. We shouldn't show too much.

"Interesting ... complexion," Scorion says. He jerks back and asks Sparik something in Dwarvish. My guide holds up his talons in peace, speaks urgently (I can hear the name

Violet), and snatches a jingling pouch from his bag. He hands the money to the dwarf and narrows his eyes sincerely.

Scorion looks between the bag and me, sighs, and takes the money. He searches through the quaint front desk as he says, "Anyway, you two can stay here as long as ye need. We have no others of your kind here at the moment. But we're hospitable. I can place you in room three. Room two is occupied."

"I thought no one had their horses or Umerz here tied to the lot," Sparik says, perusing the rabbits sitting on the mantel.

"Room one is for my sister and I. Room two is for a Giddrathian dragoness." The dwarf puts a hand to his forehead. "She has such an incredible story; you won't believe it. So tragic, too. I suggest you ask 'er about it, but she may be a bit … hesitant."

"That's fine," Sparik says. "We just need to sleep and recharge for our journey tomorrow. I don't suppose you have any food to spare?"

A sharp knock on the door makes Scorion smile. "We have quite the exquisite meal being prepared." He prances to the door and reaches for the knob. "Acacia? Are ye home?"

The door slams open, and a stocky dwarf with bristling yellow hair carries in two ducks, both with blood dripping on the floor. *Exquisite? Really?* "Hmph."

"Ey, I just cleaned the carpet!" At the Dwarvish rasping of Acacia, Scorion hushes her. "And for the courtesy of our guests, I ask that you speak in Kaozari."

"You should be happy I got dinner. Woodlund is probably hungry, and it took all night to find these suckers. Guests? We finally have Kaozari guests?" She looks in our direction and raises a brow. "You put 'em in room three, right?"

"Yes."

"Thatta boy." She moves the ducks to one hand and slaps his back with the free one. "Let's head to the kitchen. We shouldn't let our guests slip on the floor."

When the siblings leave, Sparik turns to me. "You'll be fine, right? We can ask for some blueberries instead of the duck. This area is famous for them. Don't worry, they're the farthest from small here."

"How about … you ask?"

"That's fine with me. We need to have a full stomach to clear our names." He pulls his heavy cloak tighter and walks across the room.

I follow him and notice in my peripheral vision a twitch of movement. The door next to the kitchen has a sign with a moon carved on it, but the ajar door next to (what I assume is) the sibling's bedroom leads into room two.

I glance through the crack and spy a thin, middle-aged, elegant Giddrathian in a white button-up shirt tattered along the spine. She stares up at the ceiling cracks. My eyes linger a little too long as Acacia barks at me to come in.

Chapter VI

The duck's glossy eyes floating in the stew stare back at me, and I keep a straight expression to hide my rolling disgust. The huntress sits on the other end of the table and fiddles with her thumbs. She meets my gaze and watches for any movement through her thick glasses. I give her a cheeky grin, quickly ask Sparik for a complimentary Kaozari phrase, and sniff the broth.

"Ah, it smells so– OH." I gag and turn to my right to cough. That stench burns my nostrils like a forest fire. Those duck eyes are taunting me. What measly, gross organs.

"This is a Renyre delicacy," Acacia says. "Hmph, if you don't like that, what would you like? Huh? The berry garnish on the left?" She chuckles.

My ears prick up. "Berries?"

"Duck and berries, I could eat that forever and ever," Scorion says, self-indulgently. "Speaking of eating, should we wait for Woodlund to join us?"

"She should be here by now. Knock on her door again." Scorion leaves, and his sister groans at the sight of the stew. "I asked him not to put bones in mine." She dips her fingers into the yellowish broth, picks out bones from the flippers, and plops them into Scorion's stew. "See how he likes it."

I scrunch up my nose. *Now is an opportunity to ask a cultural question about their hygiene: Why?* I lean over to ask Sparik for a translation, and he gives it to me. He realizes I might ask Acacia the question, and he hisses at me not to do it. "I have to know, alright?" I turn to her. "Acacia, didn't you clean your hands?" I ask. Sparik frowns.

The dwarf adjusts her glasses and narrows her violet eyes. "*Dargoem*, of course I did. I take pride in taking care of myself and whoever comes around here for safety … whether they are grateful for it or not. I can be clean and spiteful at the same time. *Scorion, maniel!* Goodness gracious."

At Acacia's command, the dwarf leads in the tall Giddrathian from before. She has changed her shirt to one without rips that show her thick silver necklace. Woodlund meets my gaze, turns, and double takes at me. Sweat drips down from my fur spine as Sparik eyes her reaction. "May she sit next to you, Violet?" Scorion asks. "What a beautiful name, by the way."

Woodlund lowers her head and composes herself. I nod, and the dragoness slips behind me, pulls out a chair, and sits. She fidgets a little before she sighs, perhaps to make herself more comfortable.

"*Raea*," I greet in Kaozari. If she is a refugee, there is a heightened chance that she speaks the language I'm using. Maybe her kingdom ostracized her for siding with the enemy, so she came *here* to find support.

She bows her head, a light glimmering in her turquoise eyes. She turns to her meal, and I eat the berries from the edge of the wooden plate. *Woah.* I beg Sparik to give me another translation.

"Oh, no, not again. We need to be on Acacia's good side if we are to ask for help."

"No, I was going to ask her about these berries. They're magnificent, and I must have more." I tack on a "please."

Sparik sighs, sets down his spoon, and tells me what to say. After repeating the sentence a couple of times under my breath, I whip to Acacia and smilingly tell her how sweet and delectable the blueberries are.

At this, her face cracks a smile. "Ah, ye like those? Hey, I'm glad there's *something* you like here. Take more from the center of the table." My plate is soon piled high with berries. My day has gotten immensely better. "I can't get too mad at you for liking flora more than fauna. Now, what brings you two 'ere?"

Sparik straightens his posture. "We are two dragons looking for an official signature from Hyrr Varsunynth the Unassailable approving our diplomatic immunity. As two, meager, unimportant ambassadors sent from Advisor Faolani himself, we need to speak with her council more about …" He gulps. "Increased weaponry on the western front."

Scorion gasps. "How can ye say that's not important? And from Faolani himself?" He thinks. "Say, can you tell him something for me?"

Sparik tilts his head. "What?"

"Can ye tell him *exactly* where he can stick his sword after us Renyrians are done with him?" Scorion slams the table and boisterously laughs. Acacia chuckles. Sparik barely can hold himself together and laughs as well.

"I will, I will," Sparik says through hiccups. "Say, if I can be honest with you two–" he realizes Woodlund is still there as she silently pokes at her shredded duck breast– "you three … This is a ridiculous mission to begin with. We just want to get there and back to our families. I mean, we can't bring ourselves to speak Giddrathian or Dwarvish right now. Dare I say, it's the perfect storm. The situation is already despicable, isn't it?"

"All that political mumbo jumbo is too much for me," Acacia says, yawning. "We just want good dragons to be safe, like you two. If this mission is so important, then you should probably leave as soon as morning breaks."

"That's a good plan. Now, is there anything we should be aware of when Violet and I reach Giddrath's lair?" Sparik asks, leaning on the table. "Is there an important event coming up that we need to plan for? A particularly tense situation we need to be considerate of in order not to further anger an already angered Advisor?"

"Shouldn't you two know if there's something going on?" Acacia asks, flitting a miniature, silver trident in between us.

I take a deep breath to soothe my rising heartbeat. He says, "We have lost our means of communication with the outside world … A storm, a storm had passed through one of our rest stops and took away everything we had except the bags on our bodies. We were lucky to find the Umerz resting outside."

"I see," Scorion says. "Well, since the hit put on Prince Sparik and that small blue dragon friend of his still exists, Varsunynth has definitely been on edge." We hold back flinching. "I was listening to one of her speeches, and I caught her snarling at one of her council members for speaking out of turn. She won't take too kindly to Kaozari ambassadors, but if they aren't from Sparik's defunct party (or even Sparik and his council himself), she'll try to be understanding."

Fantastic.

"That's … alright with us," the prince says.

Woodlund inspects our cloaks, and her eyes twinkle from the lantern hanging from the ceiling. "You're really from Capitol?" Her voice is delicate and hollow, like a silk cocoon.

"*Haz*," I say, nodding. *I remembered a Kaozari word!* I try to think of more, and I reach a mental roadblock. After some quiet help from Sparik, I ask, "What about you? Why are you a refugee?"

Scorion and Acacia tense up.

"I was a prisoner of war," Woodlund says hoarsely. "I escaped from Capitol's dungeons and hid on a boat for fourteen days. I crawled onto Eldraith's harbor and have been in and out of public spaces since." She rubs her spiked wings. *I wonder if she knew I was in the dungeons too.* "I just wish that I could be safe in my own kingdom and not have to worry about Kaozari spies searching for me. I'd visit the Lair to ask for protection and a pardon from Giddrath, but it's been too long. I'm sure they think I'm a casualty."

I whisper to Sparik then ask, "Were you a warrior?"

She pauses and finally says, "Yes." She smiles at the siblings. "I'm ever so thankful for the help Acacia and Scorion have given me. Someday, I will leave, but they have cared for me as if I was a dwarf like them. On their behalf, I'm appreciative that you are enjoying the meal."

"*Haz, zrak mellia,*" I say. Yes, it is generous. Maybe why Woodlund was so startled to see me was that her interactions with Kaozaris in the past were rife with tension and horror.

We look at our plates and widen our eyes. "Oh wow, our meals are already finished. We have trekked for so long and worked up quite the appetite." Sparik thinks and whispers in my ear something to repeat.

"May we please excuse ourselves to retire to our rooms?" I ask.

The siblings nod and wave their hands. I try to wave my wings' talons. Woodlund watches us as we leave.

Chapter VII

Windshift only knows what time it is. I turn on my side, my cot groaning with the movement, and face Sparik's back. His shoulders rise and lower in a steady rhythm. I find that to be a good thing. Ever since the situation at the river, he has been less and less on edge. Hopefully, he isn't pushing everything down. *Well, if I was him, I'd bury every worry I have. I have a task to complete, and if I focused on all the terrible factors that led me on this mission, then I'd easily spiral. It would be a distraction, and a dangerous one at that.* He has been fishing through his bag more and swallowing small pebbles the size of a clam shell, then taking a swig from his bottle of lava and continuing.

Imagine what Mother or Stratus or Dust Devil would think if they saw this room. I know Mother would jump at the wooden snake slinking along the wall, each line of emotion and scale expertly carved into the oak. However, Dust Devil would be rather inclined toward the inanimate creature and bolt around to the other statues. I think he'd enjoy the squirrel the most. Stratus would lose her mind over the fur coats hanging on the ajar wardrobe. For me, the weather in Alpi has been fresh and breezy. I smile at that as it is a far cry from the blazing heat in Kalder. Those coats won't come in handy any time soon. Sparik will want one in the future. Out there in the mountains, the kingdom of Bilblitor looms. The austere cliffs and rough pathways are clawed into the mountainsides as if Giddrath herself created them with her ginormous talons. I've never seen her, and I'm petrified to see her.

Sparik and I have obtained a new skill throughout our journey: escapism, literally and figuratively.

He stirs and yawns, baring his teeth (perhaps instinctually). He groggily opens his eyes and reaches for a glass on the inn table next to his cot. He takes a sip of lukewarm mud that Scorion prepared for him and admires the cup. "Who," he murmurs in his mother tongue, "woulda thought that they could give me a cup like this? Not even a ring on the table. Sure, it's not lava but it is the next best option. Hm. Mmm." He flops back into his cot and snores softly.

I stifle a lighthearted giggle. His positivity warms my heart (and I find that incredibly strange). I shake the thought off and stretch my neck. The bones pop, and I feel a little freer. I lie back down and nestle my head into my wing.

The lights are off, but someone steps around in the living room. Their footsteps are heavy, stumbling, and unfamiliar, and they find their place in front of our door. They stop, pause, and fade away. A different door squeaks open, and they walk inside. Silence. *Yeah, I'm not dealing with that. We're out of here.*

"Sparik, Sparik," I say, hopping down from my cot and poking Sparik's back.

"Ugh … Hm? What?"

"Someone is out there. They stopped by our door for a full two minutes and walked away through another door. The lights are off. Are we able to go?"

"We'll leave in the morning. I'm *sure* it's probably just Scorion nabbing something from his icebox. I saw some bookshelves, maybe he's reading."

"Fair. I'm less concerned about him. He was nice … Acacia, however."

He yawns. "That's only her personality, I bet. She can definitely cook a fantastic stew." He smiles hungrily and frowns. "Honestly, I'm surprised you're not caught off guard by Woodlund."

Woodlund? "What about her?"

He shifts to sit on the side of his cot. "Did you not notice something … off? She did a whole double take at you and acted as if nothing happened."

"She was quiet, sure, but that doesn't mean something was *off*. She only spoke about the trials she went through. Say, do you ever remember imprisoning her?"

He leans in and lowers his voice. "I stared at her the whole time she came in for dinner."

"I noticed."

"Yes, I did recognize her. She didn't recognize me, so there's no problem here as long as we don't create one. Let's go to sleep, get up, and leave."

"Why, why did you throw her in prison?"

"I…" He stops, searching the walls, maybe for an answer. "I can't remember."

"You can't remember trapping an innocent Giddrathian in your dungeons? I've been down there for two weeks. I know how awful it is."

"No, no, no. It's not that at all," he says softly, and my fur slowly ceases to bristle. "Let me explain. Have you ever looked at someone and thought you recognized them, but you can't find a scenario in your brain that says you ever knew them? They look familiar … but they're a total stranger?"

"Never."

"Well, that's how I felt when I saw her. She said she was a warrior. She might've been part of Eirwen's ambush. Lots of dragons were thrown in prison that day." He grasps his mane, and his breath becomes shorter. "Some weren't lucky."

To change the subject, I say, "Well, in case that suspicious Giddrathian comes into our room, let's make a plan to escape." I stand and look around for any windows. I suppose the dwarves made a strategic decision not to have any windows in the Kaozari room. The last scenario they would want is for their refugees (and, by extension, their taboo efforts for peace) to be discovered.

I turn to the door. If we walk out there, the stranger (perhaps the dwarves, but maybe even Woodlund) will definitely see us. The goal is to not let anyone see us. Still. One way in, one way out.

"Let's try making a loud scene. We could shake the cots or the wardrobe or something, run and hide somewhere and close to the door, let Woodlund or whoever is out there dig around, and dip out behind her. We can pay a reasonable amount (I think Windshift gave me some Giddrathian currency), take our Umerz, and run until we reach the Lair."

"I don't believe the dwarves will take any canu or kana. On the sign, they were clear about their hosting being a benevolent effort, not one that necessitates a payment."

"Why'd you pay Scorion when we arrived?"

"Because he saw your scales weren't of a fire dragon origin. I feared he'd turn us away."

"Ah." *That was close.* "We got what we wanted: information and rest. Do you feel well rested?"

He stretches his wings halfway. "Sort of."

"Let's do it." I walk over to the opposite side of the bedroom toward the wardrobe.

"I have a question."

I look up at Sparik. "What is it?"

"You seem to find escaping easy for you. Even if we don't need to right now, you jump at the chance to leave. I'm simply curious about … where your concern comes from."

Shame submerges me. *If I tell him, he will be disgusted. He may leave me here and escape on his own. I'll be left to my devices.*

"What's the matter?" He asks.

"I'm afraid to tell you."

He walks over and sits in front of me. "Your reasoning can't be that poor."

"Well, I've had to escape many times in my life. The times I've had to stay and face the danger, I've gotten hurt." Feeling the absent scar from Tornado with my tongue, I continue. "At my job, when things get dark, I leave as soon as I can."

His face grows worried. "You said you were a student."

"I am. I am. Only, students get paid nothing in my kingdom. I read some books that detailed high paying jobs, and one of them that was the most attainable for me was," I say, lowering my head, "being an escort."

He widens his eyes. *Do I sense movement? Is he going to lash out? Is his fist clenching?* Nothing. "Please, continue. What do you mean 'escort'?"

"I found a brothel and got hired. I've been serving there for the past two years by accompanying bankers, artisans, officers, and the sort, to events, balls, you name it. It's n-not what you think, though. I made a promise to myself." My feathers rise with my heartbeat. "I wouldn't and will not give myself to any stranger or beast that I would encounter. I already had everything else stripped from me except my family and my dignity. I intend to keep both of those things.

When my client asks me to join him back to his estate or an inn, I finagle my way out of going with him. 'My mother wants me to do chores.' 'My father needs me to cook.' 'Sorry, my dog is sick.' I don't even have a dog. The high society wyverns, not only my clientele but every single one of those pigs … they don't want to hear if you're feeling tired or if you don't want to. They want their needs fulfilled regardless of what you have to say.

The rest of us are tired of it. We're good at escaping, but we're tired of it." I make eye contact with Sparik, finally, tears brimming in my eyes. "That's why I'm good at escaping. Not because I want to, but because I have no choice. We're going to get those vials, so no one has to escape ever again."

The floorboards creak, and I lower my head once more.

Sparik nods slowly. "I'm sorry all of that has happened to you. I can only imagine what it's been like for you and every victimized wyvern in Petrichor. I want you to know that I do not respect you any less– Hey, look at me." I can't believe I told him everything. "Look at me."

Fine, I'll look at him. I raise my head, and our eyes lock.

His voice is like a petal falling on a placid lake. "I don't respect you any less. I will not shame you. I will not demean you for any decisions you have to make for your family or yourself. It's inspiring that you have that amount of power in you. I will help you in every step of the way. From here, to the Lair, and beyond. Do you hear me?"

The warmth in my cheeks spreads. "Yes."

"You deserve to live freely. You deserve that, and I will help you. I appreciate you felt comfortable around me to tell me the details in your life that are difficult to share. I will continue to respect you." He smiles, and his golden and blue eyes glimmer with something I haven't seen in a male dragon: care. "I don't see any reason as to why I wouldn't."

I smile too. I don't feel shame or Windshift's storm clouding over my shoulders. Sparik is worthy of my trust and respect. He may be a Kaozari, but that means nothing anymore. What matters is that he is good. And good for me.

Someone knocks on the door. We both jump and return to our beds. I whip the paper-thin cloth blanket over my scales while Sparik hides his face. The door opens, and I peek out and see Acacia leaning on the door frame. "Meeting in the living room. Come out when you're ready. We'll be waiting." She closes the door behind her.

We slowly lift off our blankets, look at each other, and collect our belongings.

In the living room, Sparik and I stand next to the wall in front of the soot-covered hearth, the embers glowing. Scorion tries to move his chair close to Woodlund and Acacia while remaining balanced; the rug is angled diagonally but fails to hide the duck blood stain on the wooden planks. He moves behind Woodlund's chair instead.

"I'm sorry for waking you up late in the night. You all need your sleep for a long trek to the Lair. Something came to our attention about half an hour ago that we thought you would be open to hearing. Woodlund, take it away."

Sparik and I give each other a furtive glance.

The Giddrathian fidgets in her seat, narrows her eyes to herself, and faces us both. The ceiling lantern illuminates her twisted, ivory horns. "I want to come with you to the Lair."

Chapter VIII

"What?" The rhetorical question comes from the both of us.

"Let the dragoness speak," Acacia says.

Woodlund clenches and relaxes her talons. "Remember when I said that I wanted Giddrath's pardon and to return to the Giddrathian soil? I believe I can do that with you."

Sparik straightens his posture. "How do you aim to work with us?"

"Well, what I was thinking was that I could come with you to Giddrath's throne room and show her and the council that I've escaped. They'd pardon me and let me live with them again." She smiles and chuckles softly. "I could see my family again. You two have no idea how much I've missed them … my sisters, my mother, and Giddrath, it's a miracle I haven't forgotten what they look like." A pang in my chest tells me the situation is all too familiar. I should've packed at least a picture of my own family. All I have left is my memory and my hope. So does this dragoness unless we help her. "If you don't mind me saying, I thought about how this would help you."

The prince's voice becomes more polished and perfected as if scheduling a meeting with a secretary when he says, "We believe your pursuit for pardon is admirable. All war comes at costs, and one of those many costs is the estrangement of family and loved ones. We respect your request."

"That sounds like a no," she says. Acacia glowers.

Sparik clicks his tongue. "Not necessarily, Woodlund."

"I understand that I'm another mouth to feed and more baggage to add on your trek. If the council sees me with you, I'd bet plenty of coins that they'd think more highly of you. Acacia and Scorion have been going above and beyond to help me, but I know I'm weak. Down in those dungeons, I barely ate a morsel. And if I'm being tended to by two, kind Kaozari ambassadors such as yourselves, going against the grain, I'm sure Giddrath will trust you more."

That all works ... but what are we going to do when she finds out we're not ambassadors? What about Sparik? What in the world will she do if she finds out I'm a wyvern?

"Hm," Sparik says, stroking his chin. "I believe you made an interesting point. Violet and I will take the next few minutes to talk amongst ourselves and let you know our decision. Acacia, may we please enter our room for discussion?"

Acacia shrugs and gestures for us to go inside.

Sparik closes the door behind him and groans.

"Oh, by Windshift's mighty winds," I whine, "we're in trouble."

"Yes, yes, we are. What are we going to do?"

"Obviously the dwarves don't think it's us since they mentioned the whole deal at the dinner table and didn't confront us."

"Right, I saw some crumpled news flyers in the trash bin in the living room," he says. "I thought I caught my name in the corner."

"Either they know and they're setting us up, or they have no idea."

"Woodlund might be a part of it too. Our– *my* forces threw her into those dungeons. If she discovers my true identity, she might kill me on her own, without Varsunynth's blessing."

"Maybe me too if she knows I'm working with you. How far is the Lair from here?"

"We'll arrive in a day if we ride the Umerz and only take short breaks throughout the night and day."

"In summary, it's a twenty-four-hour day." I pace to our satchels. "We can definitely manage to keep the disguises on for all that time."

"She's *going* to ask questions. There's no way you can speak to her in Petrichorish, even though that is the only language you know."

I'd get offended if it wasn't for him being right.

Knock, knock. "Ello? What's the verdict?" Scorion asks.

"Hurricane, it's way, way too risky." Sparik clasps his talons together. "I apologize, I really do."

"Don't worry. Better we be safe than sorry … I'm afraid to tell her." He nods, and I ask, "Did you see the look on her face?"

"That dragoness has undergone many trials. But–" he sighs deeply– "I think of it this way. She'll be safe here with the dwarves more than with us. They're kin."

"Are they related species?"

"No, but they are both ruled by Giddrath, which makes them inherently allies. Their relationship is a tad complicated to explain, but now is the time to tell Woodlund the unfortunate news instead."

"Fair enough." I crack the door open and avoid Woodlund's expression, which I know will sour in the next few minutes. *The poor Giddrathian ... I cannot afford to trust anyone else right now that isn't Sparik or Windshift. The dwarves were kind to us, so kind that they let us eat their food, sit at their table, and sleep in their beds. However, they didn't know us. If they did, would they force their daggers to our throats as quickly as everyone else in the tavern did? I shouldn't take any chances with Woodlund. We shouldn't.*

Sparik breaks the news, but I stay silent. I'd prefer to act as a mysterious cloaked figure (even a meek, obedient one if that throws them off my trail). I will be listening to their voices for a tinge of unhappiness.

Her face slowly falls, but she nods. Scorion paces back and forth, and he smiles and gestures to her room with a jerk of his head. A glimmer of hope grows in Woodlund's eyes. Acacia folds her arms and looks up at us with narrowed eyes.

"She can't even accompany you for even a half a day's trek?"

"Half a day?" I repeat to Sparik. Did time become shorter between when we talked in our room and now?

"You're speaking of the Grand Route."

"Right," she says. "Going down it isn't an issue. Is it?"

He looks down. "Unfortunately, the traffic would harm our time of arrival rather than expedite it." *Also, now that we're known to be on the continent, the word "harm" might not be enough to describe what they'd do if they discovered our true identities.*

Acacia steps past Woodlund on the chair and inspects us. "It's not that we don't want Woodlund to stay with us. In fact, she has been nothing but kind and helpful around the house. You might think, 'She's from the continent, not a refugee. Why is she staying with you?' The reason is because we help our own. For a bunch of ambassadors looking to ease relations between our peoples, you all don't seem open to her." Sparik holds back a breath, and she huffs. "Oh well. I don't understand all those inner workings as well as you two. I can barely read the daily journals without rolling my eyes. I'm sure you know the way from here to the Lair?"

"Yes," he says.

"You can leave in the morning." She walks back to her brother and the dragoness. "Go ahead, into your rooms. The hour is late. You'll need your sleep if you're taking the long route."

Sparik and I nod, keep our cloaks from touching the ground as we walk, and close the door. The footsteps outside pitter patter and disappear with the snuffing out of their hope … and perhaps their respect.

***

The sun blares through the cracks of the wood panel wall; I am successfully woken up. I stretch my legs in the little cot and look up to see Sparik fully dressed in a new white linen shirt and wool pants. *What if I brought clothes back home? Would anyone wear them? Why does everyone wear garments except us?*

"How long have you been waiting for me?"

He fishes through his inner cloak pockets and checks the pocket watch. Satchels burden his shoulders. "Only a few minutes."

Yawn. "Okay, I'll get up."

Scorion is pleasant enough to pack us hardened mystery meat and fresh blueberry dumplings for the journey. My mouth waters at the latter. "Have a safe trip," he says, waving from the treetop.

Sparik and I bow to him and Acacia, who gives us a short nod. When he and I trot away on the Umerz, I notice the right side of the treehouse shaking softly.

A window swings open, and the dragoness slides her head out to watch us go. She lies her head on the windowsill, and her necklace sways like a pendulum in the soberly lit room.

Chapter IX

I wonder if she's still resting her head on that windowsill, I think while nibbling on the second to last dumpling.

"Hurricane?"

"Oh, ahem, right. *Klatu*, I eat. *Klatus*, you eat. *Klat ... klat ...* What is it?"

He sighs, adjusts his fur coat loaned from the dwarves, and glances back from the trail. "*Klat*. It's just *klat*. He, she, or one eats."

"Okay." I make my voice as guttural as I can. "*Klatu verminsth!*" I proclaim, hoisting up the dumpling as if it's the severed head of my enemy.

"Well done! You'll be at least a beginner in Giddrathian in no time."

I pout. "Wow, *very* encouraging. I hope you can detect the sarcasm in my voice as well as when you notice all my pronunciation errors."

"Giddrathian is a hard enough language for anyone, even me. I took five years of immersive classes while training to be a prince, and I still wasn't fluent."

He's speaking about his experiences of being a prince without flinching or feeling existential dread. That's a positive sign. "How many languages do you speak?"

He looks up at the overcast sky. "Eleven."

"Eleven?"

"A multitude of dialects and old versions exist. Plus Petrichorish, and other than princes, princesses, and Advisors, no one speaks that."

"Psh. I only know one," I say, propping my head up on my wing.

"Don't be hard on yourself. You've had no choice but to learn only one … because wyverns only speak one language. You can understand draconic Kaozari fine. *And* you're making the effort to learn some Giddrathian."

"That's true." *I'm making an effort to learn … even if I'm not learning the material myself and rather having it being force fed to me. Wouldn't it be great if I naturally knew draconic Giddrathian instead? Or if I naturally knew anything about this world that wasn't disproven?*

"Even though our predicament is dim, I believe when we enter the Lair, we need to have some sentences prepared. Especially you. Your motivation to speak Giddrath's language will make the conversation and the clearing of our names that much easier. And– will you please look up at the sky and find the sun? The clouds are too thick, and I can't grab my clock."

Finally! Something I (and my species) know and can do! My fantastic eyesight comes in handy. "Okay, well, based on the position of the sun, it's eleven o'clock."

"Great. We have enough time to rehearse, more than enough, actually." He clears his throat and slows down the pace of the Umerz. Now we simply walk on the dirt pathway through the forest, the pools of light shimmering through the tree branches.

"Repeat after me. *Eldraithiya. Uthrain Hyurrikane, el Hyrr permetten ol pi de Petrikor.*"

I clear my throat and recite, but my voice gets caught in that dastardly rough *r* sound, and I instead whimper like a sad animal.

"That was indeed," he says, holding back a chuckle, "an attempt." He speeds up the pace of the Umerz, and we're back to the trees mechanically panning past.

"Oh, sure, laugh it up. What do all those words—which sound like the efforts of a wood saw, mind you—even mean?"

"Well, your name is Hurricane, and you are representing the kingdom of Petrichor."

"That's all I need to say? Oh well."

"Do you … want to accept the challenge of learning more?"

"Do I want to? I mean, where do I even begin? What to say, what to say. Should I start with Windshift and how he was betrayed? I should really rub it into those sinners."

Sparik slows down. "May I please ask a question?" I nod. "Why do you call them sinners?"

"Because if they follow in the talonsteps of thieves, abusers, and tyrants, why wouldn't they be?"

"Are you speaking of the gods? Not all of them are. Giddrath may have a notoriously short temper, but she is no monster. In fact, we are more than lucky that we are going to her to be declared innocent."

"Right, but what about every dwarf and Giddrathian that wanted to kill us back in the tavern? What about everyone *else* in the world who is hunting for our heads right now? What about Fao–"

"Hurricane, I want for you to listen to me when I say this." He halts the beast and turns as far as he can to me. His leathery wings pull close to his body. I listen for what he has to say. "Every living creature in Onverra has a choice to give up their soul and autonomy to something, usually a power stronger than them. They are scared of their *own* power, so they feel the need to be guided. Mostly, a fire inside them wants to beg, kowtow, and please whoever sits on the opposite side of the throne room. It's best to know whatever or whoever lounging on that throne seeks warmth and not an insatiable burning."

We stay still, letting the breeze collect and twirl the ends of our capes. "What about those who don't know?"

He clenches his fists. The fire along his spine grows and lashes at the air. "I'm sure you know the answer."

Before he begins to shake, I place my left wing's talon on his shoulder. "You abdicating your throne was one of the bravest decisions I've ever seen. What it means to me is that you have knowledge. You can discern if a situation starts to turn into a predicament, or if a predicament festers into a disaster. You know *eleven* languages. That's more than I can count on my front talons." He lets a puff of smoke leave his nostrils, and I take that as a subdued laugh. "You have autonomy, and it's imperative you don't let anyone take that from you. Not again." I breathe. "And I am more than lucky to be by your side."

The cascading fire turns from a roaring waterfall to the soft ebbing and flowing of waves. He holds onto the reins and nods after a brief moment of reflection. "I needed to hear that." He releases a long sigh. "Thank you."

My ears prick up at the shattering crack of a trunk before I can even say you're welcome. A league behind us, the tree thunders down across the path. Dust pelts us relentlessly, but I can see a silhouette, riding a tall elk amongst the pale clouds.

"Uhm, Sparik? Who's that?"

The stranger summons his ride to slink toward us.

Any doubt or illness clinging onto him in that moment has washed off. "Let's not stick around to find out." He leans down. "I want you to never let your eyes leave whoever that is."

"How did they know where to find us?"

The stranger is faster now.

"I don't know. I'll start riding but hold on tight. I'm not stopping soon." He jams his foot into the side of the beast. "*Morrya!*"

At the call, the Umerz bellows, claws the ground, and bounds off. I'm about to fly off the beast, but I hold onto Sparik's waist barely in time.

I've never ridden on any creature before my travels in Onverra. I never needed to; my wings served me well. I can walk and fly (and maybe swim, but I haven't done that enough to know my true skill). That being true, relying on a creature of this size to carry me around is an unfamiliar feeling.

After being on the ground for such a long period, the vehement rush of wind welcomes me back, a home away from home.

I do as I'm told and keep an eye on the stranger. Upon further examination, the stranger is indeed a Giddrathian. His garments hug his shoulders and legs, and the cumbersome wings arch behind his back as he leans forward on his steed. Each sharp turn jolts my body as we steadily increase speed. *I'm lucky I don't get motion sickness.* If we keep this pace, there's a chance he'll give up and crawl back to his superiors in shame.

He isn't giving up. *In fact, he's gaining on us.* At this point, I can see his horns as they ruthlessly chop through the hanging branches.

Sparik asks, heaving through each breath, "Where's he at now?"

"Hasn't stopped. Getting faster too."

"Damned sun. At least an hour has passed!"

Our Umerz flies past a sign, but I'm unable to tell what is on it.

"Hey, try checking the map, Hurricane. Where are we?"

I squeeze my legs around the beast's body to not fall off while I grab the bag for the book. I flip through the pages while glancing back at the stranger. "Okay, here. That's good; it's highlighted. We're along the Grand Route by a small village called Panok. Do you know where Panok is?"

"I've never heard of it. I do know where the Grand Route is. How far away?"

"Are we gonna have to go on it?" The Umerz jumps over a log, and the book barely slips out of my talons. "Oh, dear Windshift!" I catch it and let out a huge sigh. I balance the book between Sparik's back and my front. "What if someone else sees us?"

"I can answer that by asking a different question." He yanks the reins and leads the Umerz to bolt away from a dead end. "How fast do you normally go?"

"You're asking a wyvern that?"

"Please answer the question."

"One hundred and ten leagues per hour."

"Great stars– alright, you'll be fine on the Grand Route … For precaution, keep holding onto me and keep an eye out for whoever that blasted dragon is." Sparik's posture straightens with determination as I read aloud the directions to an entrance to the supposed route. Our robes and masks become tighter as more civilians appear.

The Umerz growls at Sparik, halting us at the incline before the valley. A cart is what stops us, but I can tell the driver isn't willingly stopping. Shouting, klaxons, and beastly roars cover up the rumbling of wheels that one might assume belong on a route. *Now that we've stopped, I can look ahead. This better be a superbly grand route if it'll save our tails.*

Well, it is. Ancient talon marks have worn down the flagstone road, stretching as far as my eyes can see. Six lanes hold different dragons who desire to go certain speeds. The farthest one from us is for the most brave (or stupid) and the closest is the one backed up so much. *Perfect and definitely* exactly *what we need right now. Thank you, traffic.*

Sparik hisses a string of curses but doesn't dare say them too loudly. I look back at who follows us (and who is at the same level of frustration as we are right now). Thinner and smaller creatures than ours slip past the traffic and into one of the lanes as easy as counting to ten in Giddrathian (I would know now). Frustration and even anger boils in my veins. Why can't that be us? Why can't our ride tiptoe past the crowd and get a move on?

"Are you seeing this?" I ask, gesturing at some pale dwarves riding a pygmy deer past a furious fruit seller.

"Yes, yes, I am. The Umerz is too large."

"What about flying?"

"Our scales will be too noticeable in the air. Ugh."

After moving up some, the entrance to the route inches closer and closer … but not close enough. My throat closes up as I look behind me and see the thin stranger holding his shoulders back and slithering past the third rider behind us.

Oh no.

"He's coming closer."

"Is it a he?"

"The Giddrathian is cloaked in such an obscure way that I can't tell, so I'm assuming for now."

"*Rinta*," he whispers, wrapping the cloak around his tail. "*What* are we going to do?"

The elk drags its hooves down the pavement as it slinks past the second rider, this one a dwarf who eyes the dragon and takes one step away. The stranger doesn't deviate his aquamarine eyes from me and refuses to blink once.

My breath warms my mask as I look at the sixth lane, where riders infrequently appear. Gaping spots between travelers signal to me how deeply my fear lingers in my bones. *I would do anything to get us down there.*

Now, wait a second.

As the terrible idea settles in, I jab Sparik in the shoulder. "Sparik, we're going to jump."

He holds back a bout of nervous, and a little unhinged, laughter. "We're going to *what*?"

"See lane three? Practically no one is in it."

"That's because not many travelers need to go that fast."

I whip around and can detect every detail of the leather haversack hanging like gallows from the slender stranger. His eyes still do not leave. I say, "Well, *we* do."

"I don't want to barge through all those carts."

"You can jump on those lane markers instead. They seem tough. Why are they so tall?"

"It is to keep the Umerz from bumping into each other and getting aggravated. It prevents crashes and injuries." Even in dire situations like this, I am still getting fed information I can't know on my own.

"Do it, please!"

"I'm not a good rider."

"Please, we don't have time for excuses!"

"This is *way too risky–*"

"Pardon?" comes a voice that is too delicate and thorny to belong to either one of us.

We slowly turn back and meet the stranger, scales covered from head to toe and tail. Down his satchel pocket, he slips his talons.

Sparik and I look at each other. He grabs the reins and judges the distance. Closing his eyes and murmuring something deeply apologetic, he kicks the side of the Umerz.

Our beast follows the awfully judged advice of the reins and slams one paw on the border between the incline and the steep slope of the valley that makes the route. The creature heaves itself up and, with its stocky legs with veins running wild, leaps over the first and second lanes.

Sparik and I can't help but screech at the sudden jerk and our sheer anonymity which might fall out of our control soon. We must brave on and escape. It is vital that we escape.

We land on the border between the third and fourth lanes and avoid stumbling into a young couple. The stone bricks are (thanks to Windshift) wide enough to keep our Umerz on all four legs. However, the lines and lines of dragons and dwarves chatter, yelp, and hurl insults at us.

"Keep going," I whisper.

"Wait a second," he says, scanning the crowd. "They don't know we're us, but what they think is that we're a bunch of cheats who wanted to get past the lines. That, or they think we're drunk. I have an idea."

He lets the mob grow louder until he holds up a talon. He grabs a baton– wait, no, that's simply a thick stick– from his seemingly bottomless bag and waves it in the air. He flicks it forth. The crowd slumps their shoulders and continues on the route. After the brouhaha, Sparik turns his chin up and leads us down the border calmly. *As if nothing happened. What even happened? Is he* insane*?*

"Sparik, what did you do? Did you wave a stick around and stop them from killing us?"

"Killing is hyperbolic, they were only upset. I'm wearing a mysterious black cloak, as are you. And we're on a large Umerz. They must think we're police officers."

"You've got to be kidding." *They'll follow orders from anyone who waves a big stick around and points in a forward direction, won't they.*

"Anyway, let's keep moving on," he says. "Look for that weird dragon, please. He might be stalking around here." He shudders.

I see nothing. At long last, I take a deep breath and feel the desire to spread my wings. I mustn't. I shan't. *I shan't?* I shouldn't. My brain is a frying egg, and after all this time, the pan has stopped simmering. I can rest peacefully.

The masses move systematically through the lines, but that doesn't mean they move at a sluggish speed. Their hooves, talons, and paws prance, trot, and gallop on the paved road. Inclines, similar to the one we quasi-arrived on, line the sides for people to exit and enter. This sort of order and precision would make Mother delighted.

A multitude of different creatures of all shapes and sizes comprise the crowd. Elders and adolescents, different shades of dragons and dwarves, even a couple of white dragons that resemble the drawings of the Surrvesians. I check to see any other ("other") police officers are patrolling the border and–

Oh no.

"Sparik, he's back."

"Oh, by Kaozar's fire," he says, whirling behind us to see the stranger half a league away on the border, "I thought we were done!"

The lane six travelers zip through like shooting stars. "We're going to have to merge into lane six," I say, judging the distances.

"Oh, no, no." We quicken our walking.

"If we can jump over all those people back there, we can do it again. We *have* to do it again. We need to make that stalker lose our trail."

"Well …"

"Nobody knows we're *us*, as long as we keep on the cloak."

A darkness crawls up my spine. Two realizations cause my fear: one piece of clothing keeps us from exposing ourselves as frauds *and* fugitives and I haven't looked back frequently enough.

Sparik reads my expression like a book and waves his baton over lane four. An elderly dwarf stops his cart and lets us hop off the border (as calmly as we can). Merging is shockingly simple. A wave of a stick and the crowd parts.

We gingerly speed up alongside lane six, give each other a nod, and leap in.

Now this is what I was missing. The wind giving breath to my lungs and wings fills me with such satisfaction. The shaggy fur of the Umerz reminds me of poor, sweet Baa (another instance where a predator reminds me of my pet prey).

Sparik, however, is muttering stern instructions to himself in his mother tongue. "Watch out for that dragoness, keep going– hey! That was rude of her. I'm a Giddrathian soldier. Talk about respect, huh." Whatever makes him move.

Speaking of moving, our little trick *has* to work now. Come on. I turn again, and– *Oh, by Windshift's gales, he is fast.*

The stranger gallops behind us and narrows his glowing eyes. I dry off the pooling sweat from my talons and hold onto Sparik.

My guide's shoulders lower, and a sigh shudders from his body. "No use, no use at all. We need to get off the road."

"I'm not going to debate you on that."

"Our Umerz is getting tired. I hope this time he loses our trail."

Sympathy makes my ears droop, and I softly scratch the beast's side. Hopefully, it will take my gesture as kindness.

We skid to a stop on the twentieth incline we pass and pitstop underneath a large tree out of sight, its branches sprawling across the sky.

"Rest now," Sparik says, stroking the beast behind its floppy ear, "for you did quite well for an Umerz your age. I can find food in my bag for you."

I stick with the Umerz and rub the spot in between its wide set, amber eyes. The gentle giant lets out a breath, and I gag and brush my nose with the sleeve of my cape.

Noticing a little gasp in the air, I glance around and find Sparik kneeling at his bag and looking up in horror.

The stranger stands by his elk and skulks toward Sparik's feet. With each heavy footstep, coins in his haversack chime like bells. Once he stops, the mask is taken off.

It's no he. It's Woodlund.

Chapter X

This whole time the stranger was her? Does she want or need our help that badly to follow us around and scare the scales off my back? What in the bowels of hell is her problem? If I could speak Giddrathian, I'd have some very choice words with her.

Luckily for me, Sparik speaks for me even if he wasn't intending to (in Kaozari). "Woodlund, WHAT are you doing?"

"I'm so sorry, but I really truly need your help–"

"We already told you that we can't. Even if we could, why'd you have to chase us like that, disguised and phantom-like? Honestly. Completely unnecessary and unacceptable behavior to follow two ambassadors from the kingdom of Amer in such a manner. Seriously, *why* did you have to act … Ugh, Hurricane, what's the word?"

"Creepy."

"Creepy, agh, yes!" He widens his arms in exasperation and storms away from Woodlund, who stares at him. Those strange eyes of hers are coming back.

"You two … speak … Petrichorish?" She asks. In Petrichorish. Impeccably.

A chill slithers down my spine, and his fur prickles up as if a cool wind sifts through the strands. Sparik and I cast each other a glance, fraught with fear. Perhaps our feelings contain something deeper than fear. *Shock? Being dumbfounded? Horror?*

Is it even worth it to hide that we know what she's talking about? I have to accept that she knows my language, but how? How in the world? Do they teach the language here somewhere, why? Is she a figment of our collective imagination, wishing to curse us for taking ages to redeem ourselves and Windshift? I clench my teeth. *Is this a punishment from Windshift himself?*

Searching for any words in the thick forest of his mind, Sparik opens and closes his mouth. He lowers his chin to his chest and lets his fire rage out of control. "How … How did you–"

"I'm as surprised as you two."

I slide up to Sparik and ask, "Do they speak Petrichorish here–"

"No," he says firmly, turning to Woodlund. "No, they do not."

"Please. Allow me to explain," the dragoness says, flattening her ears. *What game is she playing? First, she trails us without saying a word, then she not only stops being so reticent but also in my native tongue. A tongue I thought was nonexistent in this baffling world. What am I supposed to think?*

"There are very few explanations for her doing this." Sparik twists the strap of his bag. "Go ahead. Try us. Say what you want to say. For the love of the earth under my talons, let us move to a more clandestine place. No no, I'll take the lead."

She and I nod, sigh, and follow him deeper into the woods away from the roadside. A fallen tree covered in dark green moss looms along a dusty, lonely trail. He kicks the trunk, motioning for her to sit, and she does.

"Now. Speak," he says, gritting teeth.

She crosses her legs and clasps her claws together. "I am a historian and translator for Varsunynth and her council. Well, I was. I studied Petrichorish texts from before Windshift's incarceration–" to hear the name of my god from someone other than Sparik is similar to finding a legendary artifact– "along with working closely with her to understand the history of the wyvern country and our own."

My cloak's hood is still firm over my head. "Why attempt to speak the language if all the information is written?"

Her eyes sparkle with intrigue. "Actually, we found an archived essay about a wyvern pathologist's plan to help teach the language to foreigners, and he gave a full pronunciation guide." My heart hurts when this adds another layer to what Windshift said; the other species were spiteful to him and his kind *even* when they tried to make peace and spread their culture. "When we go to the Lair, we must look at it after we visit Giddrath. You two will find the descriptions very interesting. Maybe the pedagogical essays will help your own enunciation."

I'm so thankful this mask is hiding my smirk. *Me, someone who needs help with my own language? Please.* I go back to being serious, as Sparik's nudge tells me my eyes are about to roll.

"Whether or not you accompany us on the way to the Lair remains to be seen. You were a translator and a historian," Sparik says, scratching his face, "but you were somehow drafted? Did you delay your required service time from adolescence to … now?"

She nods. "Yes."

"What awful luck," I say, shaking my head. "You can't even serve by using your ancient linguistic skills since basically no one speaks it. Except us now."

"Don't discredit yourselves." Her eyes narrow. "Speaking of which." *Oh no.* She leans forward and looks up at us, two mysterious, cloaked figures in the middle of a road who stick out like a thorn in a backside. "I want to know … and pardon my words, why do two lowly ambassadors know a language so obscured from public knowledge?"

"Well, we aren't 'public' dragons. We work directly with Sparik," I say right next to Sparik.

"Didn't you say you were errand runners? The language is so hidden, the only mortal Giddrathians alive who speak it are Varsunynth and I." Sparik's exhale is burdened with history. She continues, "Please, let me come with you. My points from the treehouse still stand, and I'll hunt for you. Whatever you wish from these woods."

"Well." I look at Sparik and am about to call him his undercover name, but I realize we never decided on one. I realize I don't have to worry about that as I look and speak directly to him. Ahem. "What should we do?"

"May we please speak in private for a moment, Woodlund?"

"Yes, of course."

"Thank you." He casually picks up our bags and leads me down the path. Before he leaves her field of vision, he gives her a look. "Please, don't move."

When we're out of sight, he yanks off his mask and struggles to breathe.

"That dragoness is an anomaly," I hiss.

"She speaks like you, exactly like you."

A new thought enters my brain. "Is this normal? Was she lying about being a translator?"

"No, not at all. That's a common job. I even hire them for languages with a low speaking population, especially in southern Ióda. It's only … I can't shake how familiar she looks. And how she was able to track us so easily. Strange feeling." He shudders.

"I'm not a fan of how she's acting either. What do you mean familiar?"

"She looks like someone I knew a long time ago who betrayed my trust. I simply cannot believe she somehow returned to me. I still don't believe her claims."

"Look at it this way," I say, a stray leaf landing on the top of my head. I swipe the foliage away. "Say Woodlund only stays with us for one day, hunts for us, proves her worth, and leaves without hampering our travels."

"What if she finds out about *us*?" *Us?* "You, the wyvern. Me, the divine convict."

"If she knows the language I speak, maybe she wants peace."

"Oh, I doubt all of that. She works with *Varsunynth*. Have you ever met her?"

Somehow, that touches a nerve. "No, because I would have no way to." I pull down my mask. "Have you failed to consider a little something?"

"Oh. Goodness." Woodlund peers behind a tree and utters those words.

We put our masks back on and whirl towards her. Sparik has reached his limit. "You have a real habit of hiding behind trees and starting up trouble." I remain calm as Sparik's tall, lean body covers my face's blue scales. "You don't see anything."

"No, I see something." She hops onto the path and stumbles her way to me. Sparik blocks her way and snarls.

"Hold on," I say. "Back up, please."

She thinks out loud while trying to peep behind Sparik, who dodges her tusks that inadvertently poke him. "You won't stop speaking in Petrichorish, a dead language, even though you're Kaozari, but how come you're trying to hide yourselves from me? I sure know what a Kaozari dragon looks like. I won't be scared."

"*Back away*," he says.

"This whole situation reeks of something off, and I want to figure out what's going on." She stops suddenly and twists her mouth. Her eyes widen, and she snaps her talons. "You tell me what's going on between you two, and I … won't say anything about the Grand Route."

He narrows his eyes. "What about the Grand Route?"

"I mean, you two are trying to request diplomatic immunity, and impersonating two Giddrathian police officers, heavily disrupting traffic, and contributing to the failing infrastructure of the state. Those are the sort of actions you'd do *after* you achieve immunity. That way you won't get hauled into prison and you won't have to rely on your fire to warm you in your cell." She gets closer. "If your experience is anything compared to what I went through, I'd choose your

words carefully. I wouldn't wish that treatment on anybody …
who didn't merit it."

I wish he wouldn't give in. *Please don't give in.*

"Hurricane?"

My fate is sealed.

"Take off the hood. And your mask. We're finished.
Introduce yourself."

I feel my own freedom peeling away as the warm, black
cloth leaves my face.

Chapter XI

Woodlund gasps and looks at me as if I am a small critter trapped underneath a glass mug.

"There," he says in a huff. "Are you pleased now?"

She murmurs, "Pleased?" She stays silent then bursts into laughter. "Pleased? I'm more than pleased. You have a *wyvern!*"

Her wide eyes and dropped jaw are probably behaviors that I also had when I saw this species for the first time. Still, I feel out of place.

"M-may I please inspect you? I might need to look closely at your feathers, but I promise I won't touch you."

At least she's respectful. "Go ahead."

When Woodlund cranes her head to study the ventral side of my wings, I catch a look at Sparik, who is practically squirming in his cape. *Come on, Sparik. Pull down your mask too. You're in this with me.*

"Fascinating." Her enthusiasm is steadily oozing from her tone. "The plumage is youthful and bright, like a tropical bird." She turns to him. "Why are you transporting her?"

"Tsk. About that. Um." He stands straight up. "Private matters. From the Advisor himself." While being careful not to let disdain leak out of his tone, Sparik places a talon on my shoulder. "I must ask that you remain calm during our journey to the Lair."

"Ah, so we *are* going to the Lair." *I suppose we don't have a choice now. If she runs wild with this information, we're dead meat.* "That means you were lying earlier about the both of you being Kaozari ambassadors," she says, scratching the side of her cheek, "so who knows what else you're lying about? Who are you, really?"

"I never lied about being a Kaozari ambassador. That is, indeed, what I was."

"Was?" Woodlund steps toward him, a war of semantics beginning. "Were you an ambassador when you told us or in the past *before* you told us? Are you a wyvern too?"

"No. I am indeed a Kaozari ambassador. I have no wyvern blood in my entire lineage." He's not lying, but he sure is forgetting substantial information.

"I don't believe you." She folds her arms. "Prove it," she says softly. "Prove you're a wyvern. Take off your cloak."

Sparik is very still and casts a glance at me. As if his arms are mechanical, he removes the hood. *We're in this together.*

Immediately, she takes two steps back. The dragoness widens her wings, stretching from one tree on the side of the trail to the other. Her words struggle to leave her mouth. "You!"

"Me."

"Oh, wow, you."

"Why, yes."

"I swear with my horns to the sky … I never expected to find you here." She searches his outfit and scales with her eyes.

Sparik unclips and throws the cape to the ground. He whips his tail and widens his own wings (in vain since they can never be the same width as hers). However, the fire makes up for his lack of size in comparison to Woodlund. Sparik flourishes the pocket watch, burned with a roaring tiger insignia.

"Yes, for I am not a simple, low-level ambassador. It is me." Sunbeams stream in from the canopy. "Prince Sparik of Kalder, son of Kaozar, Brandisher of Light."

"*Prince* Sparik!" she exclaims.

"Alas, I carry no such title anymore. Perra Hurricane of Incus and I are on a quest to redeem our names from the treachery of my brother and save this wyverness's kind with the help of Giddrath." He kneels on the dirt and clasps his claws together on his bruised knee. "We ask for your help to lead us safely into the Lair, as you are of Giddrathian blood. Your ethos will guide us."

The dragoness's eyes are clouded and narrowed. "Yes, *that* talking point right there is what I brought up back at the treehouse."

"Ah. Yes. Ahem, anyway, as long as you tell not a soul our identities save for Giddrath herself, we will let you accompany us and return to the Lair for you to resume your duties as historian."

"Wait." I butt in. "Why are we still hiding our true selves in front of everyone but Giddrath? I feel as if that's going to backfire."

He gets up and turns to me. "Walking in as ourselves will end badly. More than badly. We'd die. Death. One step in the lobby, *boom*, arrow in our throat. Not even a burial–"

"I think I get it," I say, eyeing Woodlund, who shifts back and forth from one foot to the other.

"Hm, you make a good argument," she says. Pacing up and down the road, she taps her chin and *hmm*s loudly. Sparik lets out a cloud of steam from his nostrils and sighs.

"Will you please make a decision–"

"Shh, hide," Woodlund whispers, grabbing and moving us into the trees along the path. Our cloaks slip back on.

A dwarf with bags in his arms and under his eyes waddles into view. He begrudgingly tacks on some papers to the tree trunks, looks in our direction, raises an eyebrow, and disappears down the road.

"Thank goodness he didn't recognize us," I say. Sparik, Woodlund, and I tiptoe out of the brushes and peer at the posters on the tree. Our expressions plummet.

On the left of the paper is a black-and-white, detailed drawing of Sparik with a stern expression. On the right is a picture of … me. It looks exactly like me, right down to the ram horns and fur on my head. Even to the spikes above my eyes and freckles on my snout. I have a worse expression, though: one of madness and barren teeth.

I'm scared to ask what the words on the bottom say, but I am given an answer I don't want. Woodlund snatches the flier. "Wanted, dead or alive." She stares at me and at Sparik. "This is more serious than I thought."

"Not even a ransom? Won't we get a fair trial?" I ask.

"I don't know. The whole situation is murky."

"This is more than a situation," Sparik says. "We're talking about our lives here!"

"I understand that. I can read and comprehend the words perfectly fine." She clenches and unclenches her jaw. "I see I have no choice but to help, even with this new information about who you two truly are."

Wait, she was the one begging to come with us in the beginning. "Woodlund, what's in it for you?"

The echoing Dwarvish language interrupts my tram of thought. I peer down the path and gulp at the paper-holding dwarf and his brethren coming back, pointing in our general direction.

"Heads down, everyone," I hiss, "and let's walk swiftly but inconspicuously back to the log."

"What's going on?" Sparik asks, obeying my directions.

"That man back there is coming back with his supervisors. I think he really did see us."

We calmly scurry all the way back to the towering tree where the Umerz and elk rest.

"Okay, great. That's great you can help us. How do we know we can trust you?" I ask.

"We have one day," she says, stretching her arms. "Even if I had a plan to capture or kill you, I wouldn't have nearly enough time to have it come to fruition. If I was to, say, divert you purposefully down a dangerous path, our lost time would cost me too." *Oddly specific plan there.*

"I know the roads fairly well here. I was a prince, after all."

She holds up a claw. "Yes, you're an *ex*-prince. Everyone at the Lair knows, that's why you're coming with me. Also, if I wanted to kill you, you'd already be dead. Trust me or not, your choice. Please, let's help each other." She shrugs. How comforting.

My ear twitches at a bird's call, the only noise I can hear in the silence that follows her statement. "I suppose that settles it. I wonder if we can fly from here on out."

In tandem with the soft rumbles of the beast in its sleep, my stomach growls. I look in my bag and find one, sad, lonely dumpling. "Sparik?"

"Yes?"

"I hate to say this, but I'm hungry and I don't have enough food in my bag to tide me over. Plus, we need to restock for the day. What do you have?"

He checks. "Blasted sun, I'm in the same boat. I suppose we need to hunt and gather."

"I can help," Woodlund says.

Sparik stands akimbo.

"Hey, I mean what I say. I'm taking the steps to make you trust me. The end will be worth it."

"I don't know–"

"Wait, shh. I hear something."

"Again?" Sparik asks.

"Do you not know what *shh* means? Now, shh."

The leaves rustle in a light breeze that tosses dust down the trail. We hear it: a rodent trotting along the branches.

A rhythmic whistle leaves her mouth, and three robins carry her tune.

"Right, they confirmed that prey is up there. That should be enough, right Hurricane?"

I feel strange hearing my name come out of anyone's mouth but my species and Sparik's. "I don't eat meat."

"Really?" She squints at me. I nod again. "Really. Huh, okay. We can find some berries and leaves somewhere." She keeps a steady gaze on the roofs of the tree. After a quick glance around for any strangers, she leaps into the air and lands gently on a sturdy branch. With a jerk of the head, she gestures for us to follow her.

Up the tree? Not a problem. Glad to fly again, I lift and float in the air. Sparik shares her branch.

"Does your species know about Hunterspeak?" she asks me, lowering her voice.

"No, but we could use something like it."

She chuckles.

"Oh, look there," Sparik says, gesturing to one of the upper branches. "The critter is nibbling on a leaf." A large squirrel twitches with each bite.

"Here's the plan. I go up the branches as you fly up and startle the varmint, making it run across the branch and into my claws." She looks back and forth between us. "Trust me."

The squirrel looks unhinged with its patchy fur and the baring of its little rodent teeth, so it might be on its last leg of life. I might be doing the little creature a favor.

"Promise me the death will be painless," I say. "Then we'll trust you."

The light in her eyes dim with sympathy. "Of course, Hurricane."

We swoop up into the opening of the canopy, exposing the vast blue sky with dots of Giddrathians flying in the clouds. I feel free and unbothered. We fought against practically half a village and faced emotional turmoil the size of fifty of these rodents.

To my chagrin, I lash a bit of lightning at the critter's tail. The creature squeaks and runs down the original tree. Sparik, following the plan, gnashes his teeth at its face, making it climb back up.

The squirrel sprints down the branch and leaps onto the other tree, where Woodlund hides in the shadows. Her green eyes burn from the darkness, and she grabs its neck. With a swift crack, the creature is dead.

Down on the ground, Sparik roasts the squirrel and several wildflowers with a dragon-made fire, glittering with bits of gold magic. A heap of edible flowers have their own place on the grill, so I'm content as well. Woodlund nods, impressed, and we eat gratefully and in silence. Our appetites are satisfied, and we follow the map closer and closer to the looming rock formation in the hazy horizon. As we ride, I find myself thankful to find such helpful guides and mercy. However, the tie around my cloak is tighter than ever as we march toward the belly of the beast.

Chapter XII

The Lair sprawls for ages and ages. As we merge into the crowd entering the cavern, Sparik hangs his head down, his hunch creating a different silhouette. I run my tail along the cold, imposing iron fence bordering the creaky wooden-board street. Woodlund is without disguise and leads us slithering into the mass of dragons and dwarves. The smell of cattle, herbs, and ground stone overwhelms my senses. *The scent isn't as unknown as the feeling of trusting a Giddrathian to lead us into the thick of it all. Sparik gives me looks every time she leads us down a turn, perhaps wondering why we had to return the Umerz and elk instead of following a stranger, but I act like I don't know what he's thinking about. This is our only shot.*

Seven guards channel the crowd into several queues, possibly to make security not lose their heads over the sheer number of creatures here. Calmly, but I can tell with a hint of excitement, Woodlund raises her head and meets the guard in the middle.

The armored dragon widens her eyes as the two converse.

"Sparik, what are they saying?"

His voice is hoarse. I am not sure if it is purposeful or not. "Woodlund is telling the guard her identity as a royal historian and that we, Kaozari ambassadors, wish to visit her office. We are directly working with her, she says. Latro–" that's the name on the guard's lapel–" is confused and asks for identification." Woodlund twitches her ears and looks downtrodden. "She doesn't have any. Her clothes and belongings were stolen when she was thrown into the dungeons. She's asking for the lead historian so she can reclaim her badge."

Latro peers at us. I silently thank the mud of this kingdom for being adhesive on our scales. "Hmph." She barks an order at the guard closest to her. He runs over, and they take out and flip through a thick book. Latro runs her talon down the lists on the page, and she turns to Woodlund. Holding up the book to the side of her face, her eyes flit back and forth from what I assume is a drawing of Woodlund to the real live version. She steps aside.

We bow and walk past the guards. My throat thickens with each step. Latro must be a part of a different department than the historians. Maybe that's why she didn't ask us as many questions. Maybe she would have asked more if we'd been alone. Maybe she knew nothing about the affairs of historians (not that I know much either). *I can theorize all I want; what matters is that it worked! But, for how long?*

Torchlights glow on the dark stone walls as the hall becomes narrower. Only a few civilians come with us past the security guards. I find myself reverently admiring the carvings and gold embellishments on the walls. Deer, fish, and birds circle around on the left wall with Giddrathian dragonesses flying and running alongside the fauna. Greenery and elegant flowers border the art.

However, on the right side, scenes of violent war juxtapose peaceful nature. Dwarves in cumbersome helmets fight alongside the dragons, stabbing and firing at frightening enemies. I'm waiting for the expected anti-Kaozari propaganda, which comes in full force at the end of the adorned tunnel.

A muscular Giddrathian towers over the enemy forces like a war memorial with gnashing teeth. Her eyes and claws mercilessly bore into the hearts of the fire dragons. She moves like a juggernaut, eliminating every force around. Impaled by her tusk is a young Kaozari soldier, flailing like an animal bleeding out. She roars, oh how she roars.

My eyes fall to the name plastered on the bottom: Hyrr Varsunynth.

Is this even art? No, it's not. It's a warning. If we make one wrong move, my fate may be worse.

The heavy doors swing open, and Woodlund, Sparik, the crowd, and I usher ourselves into the lobby.

I can't believe I need to put in effort to see the other side of the cavern. Black columns covered in vines reach from the vast marble floor, populated with dragons of immense size. A white balcony spirals along the wall, where water fountains sprout and bleed into the artificial ponds in the floor. As we walk, I notice long, green fish swirling in the bright, blue, fresh water. A dragon bumps into me to pour more water into the basin, and I ask Sparik if we can move faster.

He leans over to Woodlund. "Where are we going? Straight to Giddrath's throne room?"

She takes time to formulate her words as she gazes around the regretful majesty of the lobby. "No, we are going to my office first. I wish not for us to barge in and seem too suspicious, so I can ask one of my subordinates whether O Giddrath is in a meeting or not."

"Should we have come here for a religious pilgrimage instead? Would that quicken the process?" I whisper to Sparik.

"We'd be a drop in the ocean that would come to worship her. I think that coming for political matters calls for more immediate attention and it's less of a lie." Also, I'd feel shameful for pretending to worship a goddess that is not mine. A part of me wishes not to hide my intentions using their own religion, for that feels … unfair.

Woodlund takes us up the staircase to the balcony, and I feel a light gust underneath my wings as I stand tall over the dragons. They don't know I'm here. If they did, I'd have to fight all of them to survive. I don't have to because my allies are enough help. What about me? What have I done? I caused intense turmoil in Sparik's life. I made Woodlund leave the safety of the refugee home. If we do this wrong, I might be responsible for the downfall of society. Please let Giddrath come soon. Please let our plan work.

The hall we enter proudly displays pinewood walls and exquisite watercolor paintings, each depicting a vibrant, pastoral scene. A happy family lives in the sturdy redwood trees in a tableau next to a door Woodlund stops at. The knob is ornate with gold leaves circling around the base.

She tries the door and widens her eyes. "It's unlocked. Hm … Oh, this is my office," she says. We follow her into a dimly lit room, completely empty save for a series of hanging orange lights and a wrinkled map of Onverra. She closes the door behind us.

If she is a historian for Petrichor, I wonder … I bolt over to the map and search for any remnants of my kingdom. Around the papyrus are scrawled notes, scattered in the empty ocean separating the continents. I would give my feathers to understand them.

Can I even ask? That's not why I'm here. My heart begs to know what they know of me. I turn to ask her what they say but get interrupted by a knock.

The voice behind the door grumbles (I assume to be let in), and Woodlund looks at us, fraught. Sparik nods under his hood and asks her to relay whether Giddrath is busy at the moment.

A spry dragon in a white jacket that lumps around his figure jolts at the door opening. He drops his bucket and mop and peers at Woodlund.

"Woodlund? *Atus*?" He bows his head frantically and rambles on in Giddrathian.

She widens her arms and apparently says, "Yes, after all this time, I have escaped. Please tell O Giddrath that I found my colleagues in the woods, and I need to speak with her right this instant. As soon as possible, I must have the kingdom know that Woodlund is back. Also, please refurnish my room."

"My apologies," the servant says. "For she is very occupied at this moment. I suppose she'll be able to speak tomorrow." He leans forward. "Many things have happened in the Lair since you were incarcerated."

"Oh, really? Goodness, I mustn't bother her when she is already so preoccupied."

"No, I'm afraid not. Well, I'm happy to hear you're alive after all this time. I'll leave you alone and then clean in an hour. Do you want any water?"

At a clandestine shake of the head from Sparik, she says, "N-no, thank you."

"Please, have a blessed day."

"Blessed day to you." She closes the door and shrugs. "I don't think we can do it today."

"This is outrageous," he says. "We've been traveling for so long; we couldn't have come here for nothing."

"I mean, we could wait." I shake my head. "Wait, no. What we have to say is urgent. I don't think our innocence and Woodlund's pardon can wait. We have to walk in."

"During a meeting?" Sparik's ears prick up.

"What if they're talking about us? Right as they say they want to murder us for the thousandth time, we walk in and proclaim our true identity."

"We're sort of handing ourselves over on a silver platter at that point," he says.

Hmph. "You two have me," she says, smiling as much as she can.

Hm. "We have a dragoness brought back from certain death." Sparik looks at the ceiling. He says, "Okay. Instead, let's sneak in. We'll get caught up with the guards who don't and won't understand the situation, and that'll be messy for all three of us. Let's avoid them altogether."

We nod, assign Woodlund to find a less evident way to enter the throne room, and exit the office (not without me snagging the map and folding it into my bag). Woodlund agreed to help translate it when tensions die down. "It can be a sort of victory translation meeting," she muses. "We'll be fine." She marches down the hallway, takes a left, and takes a right. I attempt to spy in front of her, wondering when she'll stop.

Eventually she takes notice of a golden door, guarded by two dwarves. We can't just waltz in there, so the group and I ponder what to do next.

I spy a shrubbery in the corner of the hall, and I send some electricity over to the plant. Hastily, the dwarves rush over to extinguish the fire I started. When they return, we're already inside as if nothing happened.

Shelves and shelves of tanks line the huge room. In those tanks I see eggs. Eggs? Is this the incubation room?

A timer above the doorway counts down from two minutes.

"Did you mean to lead us into this room, Woodlund?" Sparik asks in a hushed voice.

"Yes, I'm sure there's a secret entrance here," she says.

While looking behind the shelves along the walls, I inspect each egg in the tanks. They have awfully large shells and spikes coiling from bottom to top. Varying from brown to yellow to even green, the eggs have the semblance of a durian fruit. They rest on top of leaves and little mounds of dirt as the red light softly bathes the shell. The remote controlling the light at the top of each tank has millions of buttons. Thinking back to technology, I feel a pinch of dread in my veins.

"What does that timer mean?" I point to the corner. Now it says one minute.

"I've never been in this room during my visits," Sparik admits. "What do you think?"

The Giddrathian says, "I don't know. We have to do something."

"Well, you said you meant to lead us into this room."

"Yes, but I never said I knew it was the incubation room."

We're wasting seconds by quibbling, but Sparik has a point.

"Unborn hatchlings are in here," I say. "They wouldn't do anything dangerous once the minute counts down. Plus, I saw the budget the council must've put into this room."

Thirty seconds.

"Let's hide and see what happens." Sparik nods with his decision and ducks behind one of the tanks. We follow suit right next to him, and I notice a vent underneath where I'm sitting.

"The worst that could happen is that someone could come in and check the eggs," Woodlund says, smushing against my back.

Sparik shushes her as the timer beeps melodically. On cue, an elderly dragoness strolls through the rows and checks the position, temperature, and light shining down on every egg. She smiles at each one.

Before the lady leaves, she flicks a switch near the entrance. Gusts of steaming hot water burst out of the floor vents and hit the bottom of the tanks. They don't activate simultaneously. That means I have enough time to shove Sparik and Woodlund out of the way into the aisle.

I catch my breath, and Woodlund jabs under my wing and jerks her head to look up.

The caretaker wields a spear directly in front of our faces.

Chapter XIII

A call from a bull horn blares into my ears. I shake my head to hasten the process of waking up, but I find doing so difficult. Something wooden constraints my movement around my neck, and I know I feel steel on my wings and claws. There's no satchel around me. Dear Windshift, what'd they do?

While I wait for my vision to focus and my brain to stop throbbing, I hear the thudding of drums. One, two, one, two two. The noise comes from not just one drum but rows and rows of them. The air becomes colder even though I can sense the warmth of bodies near me.

Through the horn, I hear my name being whispered.

"Sparik? Woodlund? Are you there? What's going on?"

"Thank goodness you're awake." The voice sort of sounds like Sparik's on my left.

"I can't move."

"Me neither," Woodlund says on my right.

My vision fully clears. I try to look by my side, and only his head is visible. Restraining his neck is a large, thick wooden panel. The same is on me and Woodlund. All of our stocks are close together but not attached.

Along the walls sit a group of professionally dressed dragons and dwarves, murmuring to themselves at my awakening. Above them are sleek stalactites and vines roaming freely around the cavernous ceiling. Torchlight illuminates the green and black of the mossy stone walls.

"Oh, no. Oh, no, no, no. I think I know where we are," Sparik whispers.

"Where?" I ask.

"Look ahead," Woodlund says.

Gazing downward strikes more dread in my heart. There is an iron lever connecting to an underground contraption. *What are they going to do to me?*

I look forward, smelling the damp air, desperate for any answer. The last thing I remember is the spear pointed at my face.

I was correct about the rows of drummers, shrouded in mist and their physiques obscured in heavy coats. At the end of the vaulted and foggy room, a giant, black pit spreads across the end with a singular throne in front. The ebony and pine slither around the throne like two anacondas with roses flourishing from the crevices. On the sentient wood, someone lounges, twirling a small dagger in their talons. The growing fog covers their features.

Whoever it is looks up and grimaces. With a thundering step, they get up from the throne, flip the dagger in its holster, and march towards us.

As the fog separates, the drums get louder and the chill down my spine gets stronger. The dragon's hulking red armor doesn't slow down her movement toward us. Her spiked tail levitates just above the hard-stone ground, her scales the color of fire-scorched earth. On her broad shoulder plates are two pale horns, curling toward her helmet.

One, two, one, two two. She stops in front of us and raises the small dagger again in her talons. The drumming halts, and the crowd stands.

The dragoness takes off and places her helmet to her feet. She folds her arms and leans down to inspect us. She is just as mammoth as the carvings had described.

"Well." Her voice has a threatening timber and bass. "What do we have here?" she asks, snarling in Petrichorish. "A rejected prince, my conspiracist historian, and a wyvern. A *wyvern*. From Petrichor. I can't even count the number of questions I have for you three."

"Varsunynth," Sparik says, "we need to tell you something–"

"Silence. I dislike your brother as much as the next Giddrathian in my kingdom, but there is a reason why I collaborated with him." She paces back and forth slowly. "You see, he is the most stubborn, disgusting dragon I think I've ever had the displeasure of meeting. To my chagrin, I'll admit in front of my council and you lot that he makes a point. He stays with his kind. He protects them, whatever that means. His loyalty is…" She scrunches up her snout. A long scar runs from her left horn to the corner of her mouth. "Respectable. He doesn't run off at a whim when things get difficult for his supporters. He doesn't subscribe to a foolish mentality. He doesn't steal his father's magic. He doesn't find solace in a creature like her." She turns to me now and stares.

I'm in a place where I will give any respect I can muster up, even if my body screams to run. "Listen to me. My name is Perra Hurricane of Incus. We are innocent, Varsunynth."

"Hyrr Varsunynth," she growls.

"Even though we took Kaozar's magic, we only want peace. We wish to work with you to set my god free. He will want peace as well. It'll be the end of this war and any strife your people may feel."

"Windshift is alive, after all this time." She rubs her chin. "You're a liar."

"I'm sorry, I didn't hear that–"

She whips out an ax and aims it right in front of my eye. "You're a liar. He doesn't want peace. Your god, if I dare even call him that, is a traitor and a maniac. He wants nothing more than to destroy our world with you harbingers of death."

"That's not true! We can make everything right again. He may be angry, yes, but …" I'll take the risk. "He has every right to be. Please, he only wants justice. You don't understand how important this is. All I'm following are his orders; he sent me here to put every deity's magic in my book in order to set him free. He'll be willing to collaborate. We can unify."

"Unify?" She hisses in her language to a council member, who throws her my book! How dare she have it thrown? "You're trapping the pure essence of power from each ruler of this world in … here? Don't fret about the vial, we have it safely somewhere else. An important reason remains why my goddess banished him. It seems that Windshift has put a nasty idea in your head instead about our intentions."

I try to appeal to her sense of pride. "Your species is worthy of–"

"Worthy?" She bares her teeth and steps away. "Excuse me, worthy? We're worthy of your treacherous god's protection and kindness? How could you use such vile, deprecating language to describe the power–" she swings her ax– "the might–" it slices into the stone floor– "the beauty of my kingdom!"

I hear "Aye!" from the council and regret flooding my brain. "I deeply apologize, Hyrr Varsunynth. The word worthy was an incredibly poor choice of words. I believe, as a wyverness, that *everyone* is worthy of protection and kindness."

"You're allying with them?" She faces Woodlund. "Where is your loyalty? Where is your sense? Our brood is better than this."

"Varsunynth, why do you think of me in this way?" She receives a stare. "I've been loyal to you since the beginning. I only want you to listen to them."

"I do not recognize you as someone worthy of respect." She shakes her head soberly. "To lose one of my subjects in my grasp to the enemy … I thought I was a good ruler, strong and just. My heart breaks immeasurably." Varsunynth turns and lumbers away, signaling to the drummers to abandon their post. "I will make it right."

This is going even worse than I could imagine.

"I will not be moving my position on where I stand against you two, now you three." She converses with her underlings, her eyes boring into each of our souls.

The worst dread this far arrives, one that shivers down my spine. The sound of my heartbeat clamors and runs rampant. Does this mean what I think it means?

"What is she going to do to us? Will she actually kill us?" I whisper to Sparik.

He is silent and slack jawed; his fire spine is out of control. I wish it'd burn these stocks and chains and set us free.

To be at the mercy and talons of this force of nature makes me realize how much I miss the embrace of home. The warmth, the open sky, the smell of fresh rain on grass. I will never forget my family. Not in a million eons.

Did I fail to bring justice in Windshift's name?

Varsunynth raises her head. "Now. We've decided that we will carry out the ceremony as per usual, but since the dragons in the stocks are not Giddrathians, we will change tradition to accommodate. However, this is not necessary with Woodlund." Disdain floods her face like a disease. "We will go as planned. Today, we begin the execution of Perra Hurricane of Incus, Prince Sparik of Amer, and …" She leers at the earth dragon to my right. "Historian Woodlund. All guilty of crimes against the kingdom and conspiracy."

Woodlund's eyes flit around and stay on the Advisor's body as she approaches. A reluctant, shuddering, quiet breath leaves Varsunynth, and her talons stretch and grab Woodlund's tusks.

She wrings the bones and twists them slowly, blood oozing and pooling on the floor. Oh, by the bowels of …

Woodlund bares and grits her teeth, but that cannot silence her screams. Guttural snarling and wailing flee her throat while she, unable to do a single thing, watches the violence. What greets her instead is Varsunynth's unapologetic gaze.

Her body convulses behind the stocks, and anonymous guards hold down her legs and wings. One of them gets hit in the head by her tail and summons the wood to rise like yeast to encompass her scales. The guard huffs and returns to his post as the others force her to have no release from this torture.

The bones splinter and crack with the pressure, and with one jerk, Varsunynth wrenches Woodlund's tusks off her face.

I look straight ahead immediately so I won't have to see my ally's agonized face any longer. I hear pained shrieks and feel something dark and wet is splattered on my cheek. The intense, head-spinning nausea creeps up my throat, burning into my memories permanently.

Sparik is silent. The drums are deafening.

I don't have any tusks. What does that mean for me? The mere thought fills me with terror.

Varsunynth barks at the drummers to pull the lever. The flesh and scales that still hang onto the base of the tusks she scrapes off.

Tears stream down my cheeks while Woodlund wails and mourns the loss of her bones. A thought storms in my brain: I knew her for only a couple of days. Having an ally ripped away from me like this in such a brutal way has to be a punishment for disappointing my god. From the moment I knew her, she was loyal to this kingdom. She wanted peace and safety with her goddess. She wanted to work with us.

I think back to the map in my bag, wherever it is. She wanted to help us and our cause. She wanted to know more about my world, my culture, my language.

She is going to be killed in front of us because the dragoness in charge is an indoctrinated beast.

I tried. I tried to be rational and diplomatic. Varsunynth acknowledges the large, levied crossbow molded into the contraption in the ground and hands one of the tusks to her henchman. She slides the tusk into the loading zone in the bow and adjusts the handles.

I won't let her potential be snuffed out by insanity. One two, one two two.

Two guards take Woodlund's soaked mouth, heave it open, and aim it toward the crossbow.

If that is what fate awaits me and Sparik, I'll fight feather and tooth to keep it away.

Varsunynth fixes the crossbow and closes one eye to direct the tusk to launch into Woodlund's maw.

Without a second thought, I beg Sparik with my eyes to create a circle around my body to set myself free. I snort the tiniest burst of magic from my nostrils and nod to him. My own magic might set me free but would knock me back and hurt me, which is not what I need right now.

His heavy breaths and twitching tell me he may be incapable, but I am wrong. The fire spreads before the guards can react and tell Varsunynth.

Not an emotion crosses her face as the tusk is set loose, flying into Woodlund's mouth to impale her throat, brain, whatever it'll slice through to kill her.

With a kick and a shake, I break free and lash lightning against the dragon-made bullet. The tooth clatters to the floor.

Woodlund cries out in relief. I make eye contact with her and nod softly.

The earth under me cracks with a harsh sound, and I jump, some of the wood still encompassing my neck. I turn around slowly and find the Advisor's massive, impenetrable body, staring down at me as if I am what stands between her and infinite power from her goddess.

I'll be dead before she gets that.

115

Chapter XIV

I have made a large enemy, in both senses of the word. Her tattered boar skin under her armor sways as she takes a step back. She can't handle me.

With this giant wooden circle around my neck, I have difficulty in finding balance. That doesn't mean I can't run and duck. I really need to duck right now. The henchmen start toward me, and she raises her hands to halt them. They and the council in the stands talk amongst themselves.

"No, no one will attack her on my watch." She spreads her enormous wings. "This is between her and me."

That's both good and horrible. If her minions ran with their swords and magic toward me in tandem with her sheer strength, I'd be in much more trouble than I am in right now. What I'm doing here is similar to comparing starvation to asphyxiation: both quite awful ways to die.

"If she decides to directly ruin my execution, then it's to be dealt with between us." Varsunynth grunts and wrings her ax handle. Green vines push through the cracks in the floor and curl in the air.

With these constraints, I don't think I have a chance. I try with as much subtlety to eye Sparik and nod. My chances need more magic. I wouldn't dare ask Woodlund for her help, for she is still whimpering and bleeding.

While we circle each other, I mentally parcel my energy into not only defense and offense but also a "last resort" in case everything else fails. I'm not wasting any of my power if I can manage it.

Varsunynth peers at the wood around me, snickers, and brandishes.

We stare at each other.

Carefully.

Silence fills the room.

"AHHHH!" My absolutely petrifying battle cry makes her eyes narrow in confusion. Her guard is down, which is perfect. My offense pelts her with energy bulbs like a rainstorm. When they knock her back, I jump as high as I can with these chains and kick her with my hind legs. I'm in a flurry of turquoise magic. She tumbles down like a felled oak tree.

The stone floor rumbles at her arrival at the ground. She is welcome down there, I'm sure. I saunter around to her head and pop into her field of vision.

Varsunynth struggles to open her eyes and examines my grin.

The soldiers jab their weapons at me. While I'm shoving down the blip of fear in my mind, she raises a talon. "*Chorlat*!" The crowd of armed believers stop. "She's mine."

"Oh, please. I'll be generous enough to let you surrender. Make your guards return to their drums and let us live. Listen to what we have to say, or I will use my power to bring justice." I puff up my feathers.

Her tongue slithers in between her canines, having a similar shape to the stalactites hanging above us. She lets out a grumble from her chest. What's strange is that the sound seems full of humor.

"You, a little blue songbird, want to force me to surrender?"

I smile. "I'm no songbird." Now I smirk and toss back my mane. "I'm a phoenix."

The humor is gone. The dragoness stands like nothing happened, plucks me up by the wing, and swivels me like an elegant drink at a garden party.

"Now that was the most pathetic, obnoxious amalgamation of words I've ever heard," she thunders, "not to mention from a usurper." I thought they were cool.

"I'm the one who defeated you," I say. "You have no right to speak to me like that."

"If you decide to use cheap shots to catch me off guard, cherish that ridiculous tactic while it lasts. When I'm done with you …" She raises her hand, and with brute strength, throttles me to the ground. When I encounter the cold stone, pain shoots up my chest.

"Hurricane, you alright?" Sparik yells from the sidelines.

I hear a roar in my ear. "I'm going to make you pay."

Leaves and growth stretch around my stomach and lift me in the air. They chuck me above the council seats. I glance in their direction, hopeful for any assistance, but they refuse to make eye contact.

What I can do is heave myself down these stairs and keep going. I have to keep going. Never have I ever challenged or been challenged by a dragon of this size. My sparring partner in Petrichor is a mouse compared to her. *I had no real training against her, did I? I don't have a second to breathe or to use my powers.*

Now that I'm on the ground, I find a stunned Sparik and throw my gaze at the wood around my body. Woodlund's head lulls and soaks the stocks, her eyes closed. She may have passed out or even died. Eager to help, he stretches his jaw and raises his ears.

The dwarf soldier recognizes the sparkle around his lobes, and he barks for backup. With a sharp hiss, a mace fraps Sparik on the head, and he loses consciousness. I couldn't even get the magic to come to me; we were so close!

Varsunynth growls behind me, and before I can turn around, she slams the stem of her ax against my horns. Each attack comes in battalions.

I can't fight like this.

She kicks my face, the impact making me slide across the floor, my blood trailing after me.

I can barely move, even without these wounds and bruises.

My eyes fight with every muscle to stay open. I scurry in between her legs as a magical ravine chases me, cracking and wreaking havoc across the floor. My foot catches in one of the holes, and Varsunynth deals another blow to my wings. Valuable feathers sparkling like gemstones dazzle the air in response to her attack. Vulnerable flesh exposes itself, and she takes advantage by slicing where she can.

Without anyone's help, I'm done for. One, two, one two two.

The Advisor races toward me and thrusts her tusk to gore me in the throat. Thanks to Windshift I scramble away in time, so she only gets my tails, my beautiful, feathered tails.

She bares her teeth, but something in my brain tells me she's making said menacing gesture at herself. As she whips past me, I feel the breeze from her speed flow through my tails. I hide my gasp. They're free. The tusk ripped the chain off them.

What does this mean for me? I can't use anyone's help or magic … but I can use the environment around me. Aha! I can run into those stones there to break this side of the wood, and her tusks can shatter the remaining chains with ease.

I won't be spoon fed anything, for I'm figuring this battle plan out all by myself.

"Varsunynth!" I cough up blood at her talons.

She glares, disgusted. "How dare you spit your lowly blood at me?"

"I bet you can't throw me into that big pointy rock on the ceiling."

She sneers. "Oh, really?"

"Mhm." It's hard to tease when I look like I just walked through a pile of coals.

"You're walking into your fate, like a headstrong ox, aren't you?" She picks me up like a delicate napkin and flings me into the spike.

I aim the constraint into the base, and the wood shivers on impact. The crack is heard. I grin wildly as I plummet to the floor. Oh, this is an opportunity to break the circle even more. What about my chains? Today, I'm ambitious, so I'll go for both.

I can't tell whether I'm delirious, a genius, or stupid. Each hit, each blow, each link of my chains breaks apart. The sounds of the clinking bring me joy. Varsunynth never relents.

However, once, she does. At a chop of her ax, she lets the clamps on my wings clunk to the ground. Sure, that wasn't her intention in the slightest. I revel in my enemies' failures.

I spread my scarred wings, grunting as I raise them. Blinking the blood from my eyes, I float above her. Varsunynth waves her weapon around wildly, but I dip and duck as if weaving through the clouds.

How can I find a single weak spot on her body? Around her face and neck are hard plates instead of scales. Even her underbelly is tough at the touch. However, I scrape my talons as roughly as I can. Flesh gathers on my claws. Once I spy the exposed muscle, I launch a bolt of electricity.

She parries my attack with an emergence of rock. I continue my assault, and her eyes inspect and predict my every move. I try to aim at them, but vines whip my sides instead.

I turn, snatch her bullish horns, and yank them repeatedly. This is not the most sophisticated move, but her reflexes are on point.

The end is in sight for me. She hasn't broken a sweat. In fact, the cut on her neck energizes her more.

My offense and defense are nearly depleted. Singes of my lightning and energy darken her armor but without signs of further damage. It's time for my last resort.

I summon the energy clap on standby.

"Varsunynth?"

"You will call me by my full name." She leaps and widens her mouth to tear into my stomach.

"I won't have to." I levitate in front of her face, flap my wings, and release the magic.

The light in her eyes dims as she slams back on the ground. My physical energy escapes like a deflating balloon, and I float to the floor.

Is she … dead? No way. She was just alive. I gawk at the battering my chest took. I'm still standing through my pain. Am I really that powerful? Did my motivation prove that I could do this myself?

I smile. I'll go with that. "Aha! I win. I won at last. Look at me, council. I, a measly, little wyvern, took out your great leader. I assailed the Unassailable. How'd you like that?"

The crowd gives me no reaction and of course nothing from Sparik or Woodlund. *I should check on them and set them free. We can then negotiate for peace with the obstacle out of our way.* The colors in their scales are vanishing by the minute. Beyond Woodlund's nostrils are two gaping holes, the glands inside pulsing.

"How foolish."

Varsunynth grabs my shoulder, whips me around, and slams the ground at my feet. The earth shatters around us as if a boulder hit the space between us.

She laughs boisterously. "I'm not easily defeated. I won't let you pollute the minds of my subjects." My head lowers all the way to the ground. "Do you hear me?"

She raises a talon to swipe at my eyes, and I flinch. Before I squint my eyes shut to avoid seeing my fate, I notice the rumbling of loose pebbles from the floor.

The stalactites shiver.

A crack. A groan. A hiss.

Behind Varsunynth rests the giant pit. Smoke rises from the fathoms, and a singular talon thuds and clenches the edge of the hole. The scales are deep brown with orange vine-like spikes on the bottom as if this beast stepped in the ocean, water soaring upward. More talons curl and shriek on the granite as three sets of horns effervesce into the air.

Bracken spurts from the ground and takes down me and Varsunynth like flipping over a domino. We roar at the thorns piercing our open wounds.

The eyes appear: oxidized copper with a storming war within them, never to screech to a halt.

With each league the creature heaves herself up, I see more and more scales, the colors of a deciduous forest from every season. The tusks– dare I call them just tusks– shadow the drummers, who fall to their knees and raise their claws.

Her size makes Kaozar and Windshift look like dwarves themselves. I cannot attest to the truth of that statement, for the reverence and simmering hatred I feel simultaneously cloud my memory. The agony building up in my body from the brawl and bracken depletes any sense of understanding.

Except I know one thing.

I know that face.

For the dragoness here is Giddrath herself.

Chapter XV

No drums dare to make a sound as she speaks. "What is the meaning of this senseless quibbling?" Her tone is cool and reserved. She knows her power, but she refuses to display it because she's aware everyone knows it. Even me.

Not a word ekes out of the crowd. Varsunynth touches her tusks to the floor. "*Mien tyerra O Giddrath–*" The bracken crawls off her.

"Wake up the Kaozari."

The armor protecting her talons strikes against each other as she clenches her fists.

"Now."

She struts to Sparik and rips the wood off of him. *I wonder how I didn't lose to her. I suppose I have Giddrath to thank. Maybe she saved me after all.* I look back, and the goddess has a thousand league stare in my direction. *I should also thank her for not staring directly into my soul. I can't be fearful right now.*

Sparik wakes up and scowls at Varsunynth, or what he can see of her from this angle. *Thank Windshift he's alive.* She jerks her head to the goddess and throws him next to me.

"What happened?" He asks me. "Why in the world is she here?"

I'm about to shrug before Giddrath answers, booming across the grand hall. "I've had enough of this pointless butchering. Varsunynth the Unassailable–" strange *to call her that now, huh–* "How could you bring an exceedingly rare wyvern here under such circumstances without my knowledge and decide to kill her without me questioning her?"

"She's an enemy to the kingdom. Faolani the Unwavering–" *that's an even stranger name–* "and I spoke about the runaway prince and his accomplices and how they should be punished."

"I'm aware," Giddrath muses, tilting her head. Her tusk bumps into a spike in the ceiling, which tumbles right over a council member's head. A giant leaf erupts from the wood and grabs the stalactite in time. She hasn't lifted her eyes off us once.

"I hope you can see that Windshift is alive. After all this time, we have proof," Varsunynth says, pointing to my feathers. "However, I don't think we should entertain the question whether we should listen to her or not. We've been at peace for so long without the looming threat of an ambitious god."

"Excuse me?" Sparik scoffs and struggles to stand. He holds onto his knee as he says, "We've been at war for thousands of years." The prince faces the goddess. "You and Kaozar's irresponsibility and infighting have led to millions dying. We need to stop this, and now that we know Windshift hasn't rotted away imprisoned, there's a chance. Perra Hurricane of Incus has a plan. Please, listen to her." He bows, clasping his claws together.

Now I speak up. "He sent me to procure each god's magic, pour the vials in a magical book, and set him free."

She gasps and curls her neck to look at me directly. Now I wish she'd kept her listless stare. The earthy smoke billows in my face. "*What*? Tell me everything, or I'll let the earth consume you."

Now is not the time to be irrational. I must carry my tone with sincerity and poise. "He believes the injustice you, Kaozar, and Surrveseig showed him is criminal. Since you three locked him on my continent for eons and eons, he wants to be set free from Petrichor."

"I don't even know what to say. How has your society lived for this long?"

"We are resilient, being ruled under Windshift's watchful eyes."

Her tone is not apologetic or remorseful but rather of a burning fury lingering just under her voice. She collects her words carefully. "Do you not know why we did what we did to him?"

"No." I collect my anger. "I only know that *you* disgraced him, forsook him, and stripped him of everything."

"Watch your words," she says.

Sorrow fills my voice. "Forgive me, that's what you admit to. Why did you do it? *Why?*"

"Oh, Hurricane of Incus … you do not understand." Her eyes fill with a drop of surprise.

"What do I not understand?" I tear through the bracken, the cuts getting deeper than ever. "Please, tell me."

"He was a corrupt god. He took his subjects and made them his puppets to take over us all. We had to stop him before it was too late."

The world blurs around me. Only her and I remain. "I don't get it. He would never do that."

"Throughout all these years, his frustration has turned to anger, which turned to ire. We can't bring him back. If we set him free," she says, raising her head, "he'll destroy us all. I refuse to give my magic to one of his underlings, not to mention a thief." She snatches the book from the floor and flips through it with a vine aiding her. "Ah, yes, with Kaozar's magic in here, your god has gained even more power. Don't you see that each step you take benefits him more than you? I can't let you escape." The plant wraps around and squeezes the book. "I can't let him win." The leather cracks along the spine.

"*NO!* Stop, please, put the book down, O Giddrath!" I raise a talon to send a bolt to cut the vine in half, but she deflects my magic with ease.

"You're misguided."

My head falls to the floor. "Please. Tell me really what he did. How did my ancestors become puppets?"

The sound of breaking leather stops, and the breath I've been holding onto releases. She pauses. "I feel sorry for you. You and your allies deserve to know all the context and details about what you stand for. Varsunynth."

"Yes, O Giddrath?"

"Bring Sparik, Hurricane, and that dragoness in the stocks to the throne. It may only be you, them, and I as we converse."

She looks back at the tuskless historian.

"Do it."

The Advisor scrunches up her snout and snaps a reticent and reverent Woodlund free. She wraps a spare strap of cloth from a guard and stops as much of the bleeding as she can (or as much as she wants to).

As we walk down the chilling hall, the council members, drummers, and guards file out. The leaf that saved the robed dragon still grows in the stands.

Sparik, Woodlund, and I kneel in front of Varsunynth on her throne. We have to crane our necks all the way up to see Giddrath as she recounts the lies about Windshift.

"Each of us deities create our dragons in our image. What would benefit our terrain, how would we exude our magnanimity, how would they survive best? I gave mine strong scales, spiked wings … tusks … and the power to harness the earth around them. To give back. To respect themselves. I even gave them my name: the Giddrathians. They are strong and free under my reign. They will defend their goddess and their world with all they have. The design for my dragons was approved by Balance."

"Who is Balance?"

"*What* is Balance?" She flicks her head to the dome above the pit. Exactly above her head is a precise marble carving of Giddrath herself, holding the body of an earth dragoness. An unknown claw, mostly obscured in fog, reaches toward and basks its light on the offering. "It gave me my creations. As my dragons had just the right amount of power and cooperated with their continent. Not too weak, not too strong. They may be the strongest physically out of all the dragon species, but they have their weaknesses. Low speed, wings and body too heavy, moderate to poor eyesight. Varsunynth, open your mouth." I'm unable to even count the amount of sharp and serrated teeth she has. "One prick on the tongue or cheek would cause immense pain."

"Why would someone create fault in their own creatures?"

"Balance demands it. You see, Windshift tried to create no fault in his kind."

My feathers rise. "Please tell me wherein the issue lies." *My family could've lived in a house that doesn't break down all the time. My brother should've been born the way he wanted. My father should've been healed, and my mother liberated from her responsibilities. All this potential, spat on by an unseen force. What is this Balance, demanding how we live our lives? Not even the gods can reign over it.*

"He would bend over backwards to imagine and bring into being the best, most mighty creatures to possibly exist. I still remember, after all these eras, walking into the dimly lit valley near his castle, the sun hanging overhead like a burning sigil. Each design, impeccably detailed I may admit, was found scattered across the lands. Crumpled and torn apart by furious claws. Ones with three wings, some with four heads. Large talons to rip the spines out of its enemy's back. The magic was enough to devour the world. The ground itself was wrenched and thrown into the sky, levitating like islands. Windshift tried for years and years to come up with a creation that would appease Balance and fulfill his wishes, but none came. Each design rejected.

"Until yours. Your prototype was accepted by Balance. The smallest of us all yet carried strength. The strongest fliers but relied on wings for everything, even when the situation demands not for it. I could hear the cheers and roars of joy echoing throughout the ocean. In fact, I was right here, welcoming my domained to the continent and kingdom." She gestures to another carving of herself bowing her head and circling around several humanoid species, flora, and fauna, all bowing to her. "My dwarves, satyrs, and anyone else I could persuade to be protected by me. We are equals and we work for each other. Windshift was occupied with ambition that he couldn't gain his own allies. While trying to make his own ally, he forgot what was there. The griffins, the elves, everyone was taken when he arrived. No one wanted to switch sides for a god who prioritized his own.

"'They were perfect', he had said. 'For it was The Balance's fault, and it wished my wyverns not so.' If I can recall, that was his last straw. Generations of our own dragons prospering while his were eliminated for being faulty. He was taking advantage of having godly powers to create something not meant to be created. After that day, I saw his eyes become heavier, the more he blinked the more they shifted around his face as if spying on everyone. Most of all, I saw a vexation in him, darkening his corner of our meeting place."

"After all that strife he went through, how could you not think he would be unhappy?" I ask, learning more than I could ever hope for.

"This was an unchained vexation. He wanted to take away what we supposedly took away from him. It was not Kaozar's or Surrveseig's fault that he worked hard and achieved a goal too late. A year later, I traveled across the seawater and tried to meet him by his castle, but what I found there changed everything."

"What was it?"

"A manifesto of sorts."

"How'd you know whatever you found was a manifesto?"

She grumbles. "I've been alive for thousands and thousands of years. How long have you been alive?"

I gulp. "Twenty." *I suppose that puts her at an advantage.* My cheeks redden.

As if reading my mind (she probably did), she harrumphs and continues. "He used vindictive words against us and what we built. All our hard work I could tell he wanted to snatch away. I knew Windshift wanted the world for himself. That's why we locked him away. We could then remain peaceful and never have to worry about a usurper. Do you understand now?"

My god was rejected before too. All his aspirations were pulled away, even after all the work he put into imagining and giving life to my ancestors and, by extension, me. Everything justifies his anger. I won't let Giddrath ignore it. Her language is too vague for him to be guilty.

"No."

"NO?" reply all the voices in the room.

"No. You know why? You seem to avoid blaming yourself."

"Hurricane, what are you doing? Show some respect," Sparik hisses.

"How come you said it wasn't Kaozar or Surrveseig's fault that his designs weren't accepted by some strange, ubiquitous Balance, which, by the way, I've never heard of before? What about you, O Giddrath? What's the crime in wanting to care for your children? How come there's no peace? Why was Woodlund a prisoner of war and had her tusks ripped out of her–" I shoot Varsunynth a horrified glare– "if the world is better after you imprisoned Windshift? You want to keep him away, but how was life better for everyone when he's gone?"

The ground molds and expands around my body, lifting me up and thrusting me in front of Giddrath's wide and fiery eyes. An orange glow bathes me and the rocks.

"You will respect me." The force of her voice pulls back my cheeks and my spine. "You know not what us gods speak."

My jaw clenches when the rock pelts my face. "I'm so sorry."

"I'm not so sure of that," she snarls.

"I just want an answer. You could've helped him." I struggle to breathe. "Why not?"

"You don't have to answer her rage-fueled questions. I see no sense in them," Varsunynth says.

Giddrath stares at me, my soul burns, and she shakes her head. "No. If this is Windshift sending one of his children to vindicate him, I should tell her all of my involvement." She moves her gigantic head, and her magic's iron grasp does not leave my body. "One of the many reasons the wars have started and rolled on throughout the years is the obnoxious rumor that we Giddrathians are headstrong, selfish liars. I'm sure you've heard the same claims from your stepbrother, yes?" Sparik nods soberly. "Well, I hate to say, but they are not complete lies."

Anger boils in my veins, giving me strength after having it long lost. "What did you do?"

"His designs were elegant and carried a controlled grace. Nothing that I could achieve could replicate such perfection." She becomes motionless, and when she speaks, the stone deafeningly creaks. "I sabotaged them."

"O Giddrath!" Varsunynth rises from lounging on her worn throne and dashes to her side. She gawks at her goddess.

"You *what*?" I snarl. "*You what*?" I roar.

"Silence." She lets the stones plummet. I shriek as I fall, clawing the air as if it could save me. I am caught by something warm, or someone. "Listen, mortal. All I did was a matter of raising their net blood pressure and giving them too much wing shedding. That is all I was and am capable of anyway. I never controlled them every day. In fact, the subterfuge only came in bursts when I was frustrated with his behavior. I only expected to throw a couple of obstacles his way. Never to make him what he became. I never knew he was planning to perform genocide on us."

I turn to Sparik, still in his arms, and struggle to speak. I watch his face, unsure what to say or why my feathers rustle with warmth. He has a frown plastered. "How much were you told about all this?"

"I knew she was sorry for what she did," he says. "The rest of the gods figured out her … suspicious … plans."

Varsunynth scoffs. "You two act like you can glamorize what intelligence you think you have, thinking you understand the inner workings of the universe, but you mustn't."

What is this? Do I feel more paralyzing fear? The goddess's head is as monolithic as her continent. The book still squirms in the vine's grasp. "You even stole his magic," I say, what energy surging having disappeared.

"Stole?   His   magic?   No,   no,   no."

He sets me down, and I blink the sweat and rock dust out of my eyes. "Please tell me why he believes you stole his magic."

"My magic is all my own. No trace of his power is in the Lair and Kaozar's. Surrveseig is … a different story."

I'd like to know more about this suspicious ice god creature that I've only seen a drawing and the name of. "Pray tell," I say, knowing the full irony of using such language.

"He forfeited his magic and took off running," Varsunynth says. "Now he's hiding somewhere in the mountains. His mortals have taken control of the kingdom." *Monstrous coward.*

"Why keep yours in a vial? Why present it in front of everyone, knowing what it represents?"

"We didn't want to turn into rulers like Windshift. Better to preserve the magic and be humble than become a dictator." She sighs, the cool air knocking us back. We sit up again. "Alas, amongst us, there was an expectation for him to return, some form of him anyway. He put a hefty burden on your shoulders, Perra Hurricane." She scans my size, a broodling's play doll. "I'm not surprised you didn't know all that information, as he must not have told you. Now you know."

I seethe. "Admit it. Admit that you shouldn't have tempered with his creations, even in spurts of selfish, unrighteous, *petty* anger." I say each word dripping with disdain.

"I don't need to admit my faults to a mortal. I know mine."

"Until you do," Sparik says, rising, "we have no chance." I am glad to have someone like him by my side to exude such contagious confidence. A royal, of course.

With her eyes, Giddrath searches the adorned room, meant to worship her. A reason, a plea, anything to help her case avoids her like the plague. She must resort to the truth, but it feels bitter on her tongue. She has the strength to speak, and mountains would crumble at her feet (whatever they looked like). The depth of that pit must reach to the center of the earth. I wonder if Giddrath has control over that area too. I wonder if Windshift was exiled from touching ground there.

How much do I really not know? I look back at Sparik, wringing his talons and sweating uncontrollably. *How much does* he *not know?*

Woodlund keeps her eyes locked on the ground and away from Varsunynth at all costs. *The war between those two ... between every dragon or dwarf or griffin or whoever and whatever fueled by insanity ... the war must stop.* Whether my wish is granted depends on Giddrath's answer. We need a chance at peace.

"I admit fault." She closes her eyes. "Windshift showed dangerous patterns, but there is a chance I may have misinterpreted them because of my spite and my envy. I hope you will understand that we must take plenty of precautions in case he is out of control and cannot compromise or accept our rehabilitation."

She did it. She apologized. That only lowers my heart rate by a few beats. "O Windshift's anger may still be," I say. "He is forgiving. He forgave me and let me be his messenger to this world. He just wants justice. That may mean different things. For me, that means he shall be set free and can live amongst us." Something in me compels me to say the next words. "I will say that my language was caused by surprise and outrage. Regarding any unprofessional moments I may have had, I apologize. I want you to know I found individuals here that prove that even though Windshift does have anger, it may be … misguided." I feel a lump in my throat. *I disagreed with my creator in front of his worst enemy.* "They're kind. They're helpful. Even though they don't know my deep-rooted character, values, or beliefs, Sparik and Woodlund have supported my cause and helped me many steps of the way. They care."

Varsunynth and Giddrath give each other a look that is not reciprocated. The latter nods in understanding (I am grateful for her newly discovered tranquil nature), and the former is disturbed.

"We must speak for a moment," the goddess says. "Please, move a couple of feet away."

We do, and a giant wall of stone bursts out of the ground, blocking our view of the clandestine conversation and the throne.

I rush to Woodlund and Sparik and wrap my wings around them tightly. Sparik hugs back, and Woodlund brings an arm around my shoulder as if this is an alien gesture to her.

"We're alive," I say, experiencing the first emergence of joy in what feels like a century. "They're considering setting him free."

"All of that is thanks to you," Sparik says, taking my talons.

"No, it's thanks to you too," I say and smile widely. Instinct tells me to bury my head in his chest and hug once more. In this murky cave, I feel bliss at last.

Oh. We're forgetting someone. We release and finally look at Woodlund once the tension settles. Her face is caked in red blood, and the light in her eyes has dimmed. The wound sullies their tattered shirt and breeches.

"My goodness. Please, let's sit back down," Sparik suggests. On the cold floor, she rests her head on my tails for something soft. "You must have lost a large amount of oxygen in your head, no doubt. How are you feeling?"

"I don't feel anything." She bursts into tears, and we hold her. She claws where her tusks used to be and wails when nothing is there. What made her a Giddrathian is gone. *Not quite. She has her strength. She still lives. Through the dungeons, the wild forests, and now here. I think she's unkillable. Something is driving her to stay alive.*

The stone wall disappears as if it is a piece of paper that Giddrath burns from the top down. Silence fills the echoing mountain hall.

"Through the cliffs and gallery roads of Bilblitor to the Surrvesian capital of Lagon, you will negotiate with King Teirac and his council of mortals for and retrieve the final vial," Giddrath booms. "For you are no longer fugitives, but allies."

Finally! We even have a goddess on our side. I look over to Sparik and Woodlund to celebrate, but this is not the time for them.

Varsunynth marches to and hands me the book, the leather wrinkled and cracked. "The magic lies within," she says as if holding back a blast of earth magic herself.

To prove her wrong, I flip through and instead find the modern Giddrathian sketches. Knowing what I know now, were the other drawings from Windshift's castle old drafts of the species that were accepted by Balance? That might be why they changed drastically. *Maybe to separate themselves from Windshift's legacy. I've learned that historically, walking on four legs is associated with treason.*

"Alright. I will send with you a fleet of my best soldiers to Lagon. They will guide you and protect you. Woodlund can return to her occupation here, and Prince Sparik can find refuge in our castle. Varsunynth and the rest of her guards will take care of you." I can only imagine her reaction to finding out she must stay with me the whole journey. Woodlund's reaction is laced with horror.

"Why can't Sparik and Woodlund join me?" I ask.

"This is a journey for you solely, a wyvern, and my dragons and dwarves will protect you," Giddrath says assuredly.

"You're saying I can bring anyone I would like to protect me."

"Anyone that can provide for our team. Tsk, and you," Varsunynth says, leaning on her throne.

"I would like Woodlund and Sparik to come with me," I say. "Once she heals, Woodlund can study more about Petrichorish culture from firsthand experiences and deepen and further expand upon her work. Sparik is also an excellent navigator. And confidant."

"As long as they stay in eyeshot and in the caravan unless ordered, you can bring them," Giddrath says. Varsunynth glowers.

"I have one other plea," I say. They nod. "Care for Woodlund. Medical care." I corner Varsunynth. "What you did to her was deplorable. I have no words … other than *care for her*. Give her medicine. Preferably keep Hyrr Varsunynth away from her."

Giddrath nods, her voice full of regality and poise now. "She will receive the best of medical attention on the way."

Varsunynth is silent, narrowing her eyes at the sobbing, bloodied mess of her historian, as if they never knew each other. "O Giddrath–"

"You will help them," she orders, her tone carrying so much history. So many actions to regret, but so many ways to redeem herself. Knowing this, Giddrath relaxes, her face's spikes lowering at a lumbering speed. "You shall leave before sundown. For there is no time to waste. He has been locked away for far too long. I intend to make this right. Varsunynth." She stands at the edge and straightens her posture. "Escort them outside and give them proper provisions. You three." We look at her in awe. "Tell him … we can make things right. Now, leave before I change my mind."

Chapter XVI

As the sky fills with a deep orange, the large, fully furnished line of carriages rolls away from the lot behind the Lair. In between the transporters, rows of armored Giddrathians march sternly, keeping a distance away from the sleek-pelted Umerz.

"This is Hurricane's carriage, I suppose," Varsunynth says, opening the door. Velvet pillows and carpets line the walls along with an open icebox, jugs of water inside. There is a luscious bed that I jump on immediately. The rich cotton feels exquisite on my clean and bandaged scales. All of my previously confiscated items are in a bookcase, even the makeshift tusk I made back on the island (that I didn't even need). I feel special. "I expect you to remain in here and not to go to the other carriages. We don't want you getting kidnapped by rogues, falling off the cliffs, or mauled by wild animals." She glances at my wings and shrugs regardless. I say goodbye to Sparik and especially Woodlund, who hides her gaze. Guards escort Sparik to his carriage and Woodlund to the doctor. Before Varsunynth leaves, I poke her long pants to get her attention. She narrows her eyes and turns her head. I realize how well polished her tusks are as they glitter in the dying sunlight.

"What is available for dinner?"

"Medium rare veal pockets. Something that doesn't get food everywhere on the floor."

If she will be helping us, there's no reason for her to act with animosity towards the following request. "I'm a vegetarian."

She looks me up and down slowly. She scoffs and leaves my carriage. *Is that a "yes, I'll accommodate for you" scoff?* Time will tell.

The ground becomes rockier and gains elevation as we move along. Carts park on the side of the road for us to move forth, watching us in awe. I can't watch them for too long at the risk of them seeing me. The soldiers have acted normally. Hopefully, they continue.

Speaking of them, I hear the faint, monotonous grunting while they march along the track. The *hut, hut, hut, hut!* might get annoying after two days, but for now the calls fill me with motivation. I thought that each moment of my being here would thrill me endlessly. Even the trees would seem a rarity, and each one would be unique. My exhaustion, after everything that has happened, comes back.

I wake up to find a meal plan for the next week of traveling and bags of uncooked vegetables. As a wyvern, I can handle it, but not even leftover steam has kissed this leek's hard exterior. I bet I can whack it on Varsunynth's head, and *then* she'll die.

The carriage wheels rattle over the uneven stones on the roads plastered onto the mountains. Spots of moss and carvings of initials paint the wide gallery roads, and ravines as deep as the pit of Giddrath lie beyond its railings. The freshest aquamarine water pours out of the sides into the depths.

I want to stretch my wings and see where the clouds begin and end in this overcast sky. However, I cannot leave, so compromising by admiring the nature will have to do. But, I need to stretch. With one wing already extended, I try the other one and knock over the bookcase.

From the shelves Woodlund's map plops on the floor. I have something to read now that I have enough downtime to drown myself in it.

I can't understand the words on the pages. I can look at the map all I want and finally see my continent. Lakes, plains, swamps, and all. *That mountain is out of place, though.* Sharing my knowledge with Woodlund could help future understanding. Geography is where it all starts.

Can I truly spend a week alone like this? After having so many dragons accompany me for so long, my do-it-myself spirit has taken a vacation. Now that the Umerz have stopped for a water break, Woodlund needs a friend more than ever.

What to do about the guard? She stands by the door next to the hitch. Maybe the soldier will let me leave if she can occupy me and see I not fall or get attacked. I glance at my satchel with the book and vial inside and snatch it, paying attention to its position on my body at the risk of the bag being stolen.

I stick my head out the window and ask in quite easily the most broken Giddrathian possible if I could visit Woodlund.

"For what?" She asks (I think) while she points to an upcoming sign. On the wood is a painting of a horse bust, a horn elongating from the forehead. We're in unicorn country now (apparently that's a scary thing?).

Speaking to Woodlund isn't a good enough reason. "Gift." I had learned the word for gift (*cheleed*) since I thought I should give Giddrath one when we arrive at the Lair. Sparik said that could be an idea, but it's too late now.

The guard stares at me. She nods, takes me to Woodlund's carriage, and waits in the corner by the door. She and the doctor converse while keeping an eye on us.

The linen window curtains sway with the faint breeze as the dragoness lies on a bed as comfortable as mine. They take care of their own here. I look at her bandages covering her upper snout. *Or so I think.*

"Woodlund, are you awake? I have something for you." *Now that I think about it, the guard doesn't understand Petrichorish.*

She groans while she shakes the sleep off. "Is that you, Hurricane? W-why are you here?"

"I wanted to check on you." I take her talon above the covers. "How are you?"

She stares groggily ahead, silent for a moment. "How do I even answer that? My body feels like it's missing something. I'm missing myself."

"Is the pain better?"

Clasping her jaw and muting her hiss, she shakes her head.

Should I still ask her about the map? "How about I see you again tomorrow? I don't want to disturb you any longer. Oh, and here's a … leek." Not the most fitting gift, but I'd like to hold onto the map for a while longer. I place the food on her table.

Before I leave with the guard, she takes and squeezes my talon. "Thank you," she says.

A few days pass, and I keep Woodlund in my prayers and raw vegetables in my stomach. I haven't prayed to Windshift in a while. Perhaps he knows everything already and is thrilled we have the magic. *Does he?*

I find myself facing the window again, and now my mind wants me to process what Giddrath said. How'd she know he'd try to destroy them just from some manifesto that contains "aggressive language" or whatever semantics she used? The last time I talked to him, he may have wanted justice, but he is a peaceful god at heart. He wants to save my family and each and every wyvern from strife and misery. *Just like Giddrath.*

I have already learned that dragons here deserve mercy and stand for the exact tenets Windshift holds dear, so why enact vengeance against them? I'm sure he'll understand. He'll meet Sparik and Woodlund and completely understand.

After that butchering, how much good is left in Giddrath's heart? She feels immense guilt for sabotaging Windshift, of course, but she sat by while we were to be killed. *But at least she stepped in.*

Woodlund. She must understand how I feel. Her own Advisor is doing that to her, not even getting to see her family ...

I told Mother, Father, Dust Devil, and Stratus I'd be away for "a few weeks." At least Woodlund didn't tell her family falsehood. She went into battle and was captured, yes, but at least she didn't say she was working with Kaozar or something like that.

Not only am I potentially disobeying Windshift by allying with the enemy again (even if it is for the greater good), but I also betrayed my family's trust.

Talking to Woodlund won't calm my mind. I need to be around someone else who I won't bother with my incessant rambling. Someone who's heard it before. Someone whose mother needs saving.

I pull the same song and dance with the guard and get her to bring me to Sparik's carriage. This time, I have a piece of mountain potato as a little snack. Perhaps he and I could share it.

His area is the smallest out of Woodlund's and my own, and the bed seems the stiffest with the tautest canvas sheets. The guards wait outside. Reading a book and covered by two thick blankets, Sparik sits hunched over on a bench molded into the side of the carriage interior.

He notices me entering immediately. "Ah, good afternoon. What brings you here?"

"We haven't talked in a while, one on one. I just wanted to see how you were holding up."

He closes the book softly. "What do you want to know?"

"Have you been thinking about your mother lately?"

Sparik frowns and turns toward the imposing bookcase next to the bench. "Why, yes. Every day."

"Do you ever think that you've let her down?" He breathes heavily. "That you ran away and left her stuck in a terrible situation she cannot escape from?" I gulp. "Even though you still think about her, she has no idea where you are and if you're dead or not?"

"Why are you even asking me such questions?" His voice has an old, familiar character to it: one from the canals of Eilora, where he bound and threatened to kill me if I wasn't silent.

I shouldn't be surprised that he seems frustrated after all we've been through in the last week, but I am.

"Of course, I think that. Of course, I think that I let her down and she's stuck with my brother and father. She doesn't deserve them. You saw it with your own two eyes. She stood on that dock while Faolani and Kaozar decried me and didn't even say a word."

"I can understand. I know it's hard–"

"What do you know?" He faces me, his eyes cast over. "I never ask you where you think your family is because the question is insensitive."

"I know they're safe, but I'm worried about what they think of me."

"That has nothing to do with my situation. We must be honest with ourselves here: we live in entirely different worlds. Your parents and brother haven't even witnessed the pressure my mother is burdened with. The stares and snide remarks she gets? To Faolani and his followers, she's nothing but an insolent bird that has tainted what was to be my pure blood. Your family loves each other, and what am I left with? Please, let's not compare. If this is what you're wanting to talk about, then just–"

"I'll tell you why," I say. "I'll tell you why I wanted to talk about it, okay?"

"I don't want to right now." He shivers under his blankets and buries his head in the book. Even without touching him, he and his demeanor are chilling to be around. If I don't release this tension with him, I don't know what I'll do.

"Sparik, I lied."

An eye peeks behind the pages.

"I told my family I'd be home in a few weeks. It's been at least a month, possibly longer. I just can feel they're worried sick about me, but I don't deserve this attention from them."

"You call that a lie? Did you know you'd take longer?"

"Not just that. I told them I'd be training at the school for maids so I can work at the royal concubine. Not mending the

145

world with dragons I met only a month ago. Even when we come back, set free Windshift, and have my family saved … will they forgive me?”

I gaze upon myself in the window reflection. Have my bones become stronger, or has my face become thinner? The sparkle in my scales is dimmed with bandages, dirt, scars, and a month's worth of inward war.

“Maybe I thought I would be ambitious enough to take this world by storm in the right amount of time. This is way more difficult than I thought, and way more profound. I had no idea that Windshift … he was that fueled by rage. Maybe he wasn't. Maybe that caricature of him was Giddrath's projection. Sparik?”

“Mhm?”

I don't notice the creaking of wood behind me. All I have my eyes on are the clouds above, hiding the sky from me. “What if the other designs were accepted? To think that there could've been a different version of me. Or that I wouldn't have existed. How would I look with navy scales? Or a lighter mane? Or two heads? Would they be multicolored or match?” *Would I still have been chosen by Windshift?*

Sparik places a talon on my shoulder. “You sound like you have a great deal going on in your mind right now.”

“I bet I'd still be a liar and a failure in those worlds too.” I turn from the window and flop on the ground, burying my head in my wings.

He sits next to me, his fire calmly warming my back. “I think you had to lie for an important reason. I don't think they'll be mad at you after everyone is saved. From what you described, Windshift can be easily reasoned with. He has a benevolent heart. Giddrath just needs to amend her mistakes.”

He clears his throat but not in a way to prompt a response from me. "I apologize. We may lead different lives, but that doesn't make one pain harder to endure than the other. Please, speak to me when you have an issue like this."

"You're okay." I sniffle. "At least you remember that I have a brother."

"Of course, I do." He helps me stand. I still stumble on two legs, but he holds me. "In order to help other dragons, I must remember small things about them … You're worth helping."

The carriage shakes violently back and forth. He falls onto me, and for an instant our eyes lock.

"What was *that*?" I ask a little too loudly, my heartbeat drowning out my hearing.

He holds up a talon to my snout. "Wait, I hear something else. Above."

We look up slowly. Hooves clop on the roof and toward the side of the carriage with the door.

Sparik whispers, "I think the guards will be looking for you. Just stay here in my room, and they'll account for both of us. Most of all, let's be quiet."

A large horse's nostrils sniff the glass window right behind me, the lips of the creature flopping around like a dying fish. I find difficulty in not laughing right now, for the monster looks ridiculous.

As if finding immense displeasure in my taunting, the horse lowers its head, brandishes its singular horn, and bares sharp fangs. I jump back and yelp as the unicorn headbutts the door. The glass spews everywhere as the beast's long torso hangs through the window, the air blowing its rancid, green mane inside the one place in which I wanted to be safe.

Sparik looks around and thinks out loud frantically under his breath. He pauses and grabs the unicorn by the jaws. With its horn, the beast tries to pierce him, and I bat my wings to expel the wind to the unicorn. The beast shrieks a horrible, scathing sound and bites the glass still there on the door to hang on. Blood oozes from the roof of its mouth, but the pain won't stop the monster from tearing us apart.

Sparik summons light from his lamp, rendering it ineffective for the rest of the trip, and pushes the unicorn away with the magic, but it still hangs onto the hitch. Moving up its hind legs, the unicorn grabs onto the copper link with its dirty and serrated hooves and leaps into the air. It balances on the hitch.

Sparik runs over and looks out the door. He immediately starts pacing back and forth, stumbling. "That's not good, that's not good."

The unicorn anticipates jumping into the carriage and then jolts upward, perking up thin, ragged ears. Sparik and I watch for what it does next. Upon hearing a cry from its brethren, it runs away and neigh-screeches.

We take Sparik's beloved tarp and cover the broken glass. I hear the Giddrathian roars and horse whinnies, followed most of all by the hacking and slashing. We take cover, huddled next to each other. Ages feel like they pass, and the carriages skid to a stop. No more screams or slashing can be heard.

Someone raps on our door. We open it to find Varsunynth gripping a strip of black, blistering meat in one hand and a wicked horn in the other, covered in blood the color of licorice. She breathes normally.

"Did the unicorns attack you two?" she asks. I nod. "Did you get bitten?" I shake my head. "Good. Well, we drove them off. Our Umerz are still alive, but the carriages that are hauling supplies are damaged. We have to make a pit stop by this fishing town." She hands me the meat and horn. I frown and widen my eyes at the thin slices of fat near the tough skin. "Toss these out, won't you? The rest of the herd will track us down if we have any unicorn remnants." Chuckling, she closes the door, and Sparik and I chuck them into the ravine. The meat splats on the side of the rock, and we wince.

Chapter XVII

In a few hours, we make it to Mysharal, or in my language, Leopard's Lake. On my book's map, this body of water stretches farther than the others in the kingdom. Along the lake is a large fishing village that we can stay in for two days.

We roll down the hard dirt ground and stop by a brick inn, sticking out from the mass of log houses with stone chimneys. Varsunynth checks us into the largest, most expensive, high security room for Woodlund, Sparik, and I. *How pleasant ... and out of character for her.* The grit of her teeth when she receives the copper key proves my judgment of her right. Five guards join us. I offer to bring them a cup of water. No response but a polite shake of the head. A couple of days ago they were attempting to kill me.

I am thrilled to speak with Woodlund again, especially about the unicorns. I describe the battle and our opponent's retreat, scurrying away "like a measly rat getting its tail stepped on." On the night of, we are given room service and strict orders to stay inside our quarters, which is large enough for Woodlund, Sparik, and I to sleep in. One of the guards stays too. The rest station outside.

I slide underneath the covers and sip on my bowl of squash stew. The blanket has little, coarse hairs that tell me that this wasn't craftily made. My mother could do better.

My bed has a direct view of the lake with rows upon rows of mountains behind, like spikes protecting outward forces from invading. The water is a dark teal color, complimenting the white and gray of the lonely sandy beach. I hear the rumbling of string music and lively laughter a few floors down. Woodlund comes into my corner and leans on my bedpost, also looking out the window.

"I've heard remarks from ancient Petrichorish articles that the lakes in your kingdom are to be quite beautiful," she says quietly.

"You might be talking about … Hm, I can't remember if I visited, but my friend in my hometown loves the weather up there. It's that large one in the northwest."

"Ah, sounds lovely." She bows and returns to her bed.

While my roommates sleep, I stay up yet again. I need air. I flounder over to the window and creak it open. Woodlund groans from the corner and then ceases. I can't tell if she's making that noise to shut me up or if her dreams are treating her unpleasantly. I shut the window and leave it at that. Instead, I look to the stars. They look just like the stars in Petrichor. Perhaps this is Giddrath feeling like she can be justified in her actions if she represents a part of Petrichor in her own work. Immaculate detail lavishly rests in each league of the sky. I wonder how a star feels. Far away from everyone in space, maybe wishing to have a friend. Chained down to shine in the sky.

After two hours of thinking, I lumber over to my bed and slam my body on top of it. As my eyes flutter, I notice the tapestry hanging behind my bed, with large cats covered in shells and hiding in caves. I pet the cloth; it is void of heat but the threads glow.

In the morning, Sparik brings us warm pastries and says he can teach us a Giddrathian card game to pass the time. Woodlund says that even though she knows the game by heart, she needs to distract her mind.

In the middle of our seventh game of Feathers & Stones (one uses feathers and stones in this game), Varsunynth comes back and tells us about the situation.

"Nobody is outside right now. There's fog and mist everywhere coming from the lake. I asked a dragon– the only one out there– what was going on, and he told me about the big cat." She looks at Sparik who nods.

Well, I can't help but inquire. Leopard's Lake must mean something. "The what?"

"There's a legend that a large, long leopard with white fur sits at the bottom of that lake. The mist is supposedly her breath." Varsunynth huffs and chuckles. "I'd be surprised if Giddrath put a *leopard* down there. If I ever brought my family here, the story would scare my daughters to stay in their rooms."

Woodlund reshuffles the raven feathers behind her back. "Were you able to find any carriages?"

Varsunynth pauses, searching Woodlund's face. "No," she says. "The citizens here all stayed inside because they were afraid of the leopard. The stores and stables nearby were all closed because of the fog. We're going downtown to see if there are any rides to rent." She bows and exits.

In the meantime, Sparik teaches me a more advanced, ancient version of Feathers & Stones. This time, the lighter side of the raven feather means everything, and the number of indents on the stones is only something to tack onto for extra points. While playing, I can't stop thinking about the leopard. On my continent, we only have mountain and swamp lions, and they look nothing like how the tapestry above my bed makes them look. This is confusing me. I feel like I'm draining poor Sparik by asking him about everything. He must want me to go to bed and stop pestering him. Checkmate. Or as the Giddrathians say during Feathers & Stones, *"Attekuday."*

Another three hours pass, and I am on a winning streak. I rub my talons together like a masterminding fly and gather the bounty I won. Sparik coughs and sniffs while wrapping a blanket around him tighter. Once the wind threatens to blow away my feathers, we eventually close the window. As much as I love air, I can feel like a winner without it.

Varsunynth enters again, now with a bloody eye. She seems bored of the wound.

"Renting carriages didn't work. One of them rolled over one of my soldiers."

"What in the world did you do to cause that?" Sparik asks, bewildered. "I thought we could leave when the moon rises."

"It's the fog, Sparik. Simply because your father failed to rear you correctly is not a good reason to doubt me." He blinks. "Ahem, sorry. We're going to have to wait until morning. Maybe we'll find information when the mist rolls out of the inn's tavern. We can have a meal there too." She is about to leave. "If you decide to join us, wear a cloak. A heavy one." She's gone. *What a charming dragoness.*

Chapter XVIII

The tavern's damp air condensates underneath Sparik's fur coat loaned by the dwarf house (which was given to me for the night), and where we sit at the bar the torchlight heats the back of my neck. Where I am is smaller and rougher around the edges than the pub in Eldraith when we first arrived on Alpi. I look ridiculous in this cloak, by the way, like one of those tropical birds puffing up its feathers to impress a mate. *All my mates (so to speak) here are soldiers and dragons investing in my success.* I must not think negatively now, for I have food to look forward to.

Woodlund decides to forgo coming with us, and Sparik offers to buy her a meal of venison kebabs and mashed potatoes. She is about to reject the offer, but I nudge her to let her know she will be okay. The dragoness nods and sits at the foot of her bed when we close the door.

I get served carrot stew in this beautifully furnished bowl, with watercolor paintings of river catfish around the rim. The wool placemat has little hairs sticking out of the tightly braided ropes, forming concentric circles in the placemat. Orange droplets rain on the fabric as I sip on the stew. The broth is rich and robust in flavor. *Another ally. More reliable.*

Out of the corner of my eye, someone unfamiliar decides to sit next to me. Begrudgingly, I remember that Varsunynth was right about the cloak. This reeking fisherman bumps into me, and I spill a little bit of the stew from my polished wooden spoon. In the rare moment where no guard is looking, I pluck up the orange splotch and put it in my mouth. The thin, fuzzy hairs from the placemat ruin all of the previous warm, toasty taste. I hack out the fur ball and bump into the bowl again, shuddering and cleaning the spoon with my cloak. I never want that sensation in my mouth again.

"Hurricane? Someone wants to speak with you," Sparik says, tapping me on the shoulder. He flits his eyes to the right, and I turn slowly to see the bartender, covered in the orange goop, flaring his nostrils.

The guards and Varsunynth herself shift uncomfortably in their wooden chairs but let the scenario play out. This is the second run-in I've had with a bartender because of my negligence, and I'm praying for it to be the last.

The golden yellow dragon shoves past other servers behind the bar and marches toward me. He makes broad gestures with his talons and grumbles in a different sounding Giddrathian language, as rough as the mountain ranges here.

I open my mouth to speak, but all I can manage is "*Plencihew.*" I'm sorry.

He doesn't take that well, and the guard closest to me steps in front of me to speak.

The rest of what happens is a blur. I don't know if explaining my behavior to the dragon will make me feel better or worse. They again excuse my actions caused by my inattentiveness. I sip on the rest of the stew, which gathers at the bottom of the bowl and clings on for dear life.

As I raise the bowl, I hear the disgruntled conversations of other bargoers. They stare at me from the corner, their disdained faces highlighted by the candle in the middle of the table. Even the strangers are ashamed that I am the chosen one here. Well, they don't know me or any of us as long as Varsunynth and Sparik still keep their appearances hidden. Embarrassment still torments me, no matter the relaxing thoughts I choose to think instead.

What happens next is I see a whirl of ginkgo leaf yellow and feel a bolt of pain in my ear. This blow hurts more than what Varsunynth gave me.

Honestly, I choose not to look. The tension and stickiness of the stew build in my chest.

I'm tired.

I need to leave.

Once I'm out of there at the dismay of Sparik, pushing past confused dwarves, and slam the door shut, *that's* when I realize that the hour is unknown in an unknown village in an unknown world. Fog spreads around the pier less now but still floats in splotches.

Where can I go for a breath of fresh air? Knowing I want to stay away from people, I do the best I can do: stumble to the edge of the pier. The fog dissipates. Lanterns on fishing boats dapple the chillingly placid lake with yellow light. The air is empty except for the rustle of wind, smelling of salt.

Now, I can fly.

I spread my wings and let the wind take me where I belong. Finally. Finally, I can fly. The breeze embraces my body like a long-lost friend. I can be closer to the clouds and stars now. The glorious mountain ranges curl around the water, and even though their towering peaks must intimidate most travelers, I am not only a traveler. I am a free wyvern.

To be fully unburdened, I throw off the cloak and spin in the air. Here the wind accepts me and lifts away my pain. Living in this moment, I need nothing.

Except to return the coat.

What was I thinking? What if civilians see me? I stand out like a weed in a garden.

Suddenly, my wings feel weaker, most likely from my psychosomatic symptoms. I can put all the fancy labels on my behavior that I want, but that won't distract me successfully from the truth. My gaze rests on the beach down below, and I reluctantly pluck up what I threw down.

I toss the sopping wet coat on the beach, and when I slam my head on the sand, those pesky flecks get in between my scales and the spikes above my eyes. I am alone on this white, empty, nothing beach, the black water lapping my tails and legs. I heave myself up and move into a more comfortable position. Their dark colors bleeding into the sky, the deciduous leaves and branches murmur at my arrival.

I am witnessing nature as Giddrath intended. Quiet and contemplative. Dark and mysterious. Cold and intimate. Do I feel calm? Or do I feel as lonely as I did on the beaches of Alvoreçer? I scoop some sand and let it fall between my talons. How much sand is even here? I'm sure I could count forever.

Part of me wishes they won't find me. But there are probably a bunch of guards searching regardless. I scoff. *Their one ray of hope.* How am I supposed to be a ray of hope if my world has turned upside down? I could've been perfect. I examine my feathers, or rather the lack of some of them. I have to wait to molt a year from now and then I can grow back what I'm missing. Until then, sticking with my scars and ruined wings is not something I'm looking forward to. These wings made me who I am. Windshift made me, my family, and ancestors the winged saviors we are.

Am I a savior? Am I, Perra Hurricane of Incus, twenty years old, "little blue songbird" … really a savior? I couldn't have done any of this by myself. Sparik helped me steal the vial, Woodlund brought us to the Lair, and Giddrath gave me mercy. I'm lying on this beach because I was wished into existence. I didn't wish myself into existence. Not me. Windshift did. And look at me now, getting overwhelmed and running away. I must bring disappointment to his name. The lights still shine from the inn's windows in the distance.

The thoughts of betrayal return to my mind like an army storming a battlefield. *If my god wants me to bring him justice, why am I allying with his worst enemies? Does he know I struggle with these thoughts? Sure, he made me feel special. I am turning against living beings that, yes, definitely deserve mercy. According to him, they don't. They will, though, once he sees. What if he doesn't?*

The infinite world is more dizzying than I thought. Windshift has no idea. For once, I don't feel ashamed admitting that.

What do I do now? As the stars rotate in the sky on a predestined path set by a dragoness who knows all and sees all (save for Balance, that bastard), do I sit here and cry about where my life has directed me? Do I bemoan how this, this experience right here, is not how I planned? Hurricane months ago wouldn't have dared to imagine herself on the banks of Leopard's Lake, thinking about how infinitesimal and how much of a failure she is.

The sand lets me sink into its covers. I was chosen.

I was *chosen.*

I *was* chosen.

Chapter XIX

"Hurricane?" A rough voice disturbs the peaceful rustling of branches.

"Please. Let me be." I don't care for decorum, but I'm no longer running.

Varsunynth stands in between the trunks, holding onto each with her large hands. Her expression is languid. Out of all the dragons in the world to visit me here, she is the last I'd expect.

"Why are you here? How'd you find me?"

"The guards saw you flying and crash landing into the sand here. You know you can't be out here on your own."

My theory is that she doesn't understand or experience empathy, so I will not converse with her about my feelings. "The fresh air is nice. You can go back and tell the guards that I'm safe here." I glance back. "Unless you're plotting something–"

"Oh, please. If I wanted to kill you, you'd be dead already."

I narrow my eyes. "No, you wanted to kill me, and you nearly did. O Giddrath stopped you."

"I mean on the caravan or someplace similar. Right now, I want to bring you back. We explained the situation to the bartender, and the innkeeper backed up our claims. He apologized profusely."

We sit as the breeze swirls through the night. The waves go back and forth back and forth, and they never stop. I lean over and let the ebb and flow wade over my talons.

I shuffle away from her. "You Giddrathians really love to use that threat, don't you?" I mimic a tough voice. "Oh, if I wanted to kill you, you'd be dead by now." I freeze. Even though I'm questioning the meaning of my life, I still have time left, and I don't want it destroyed because of another senseless comment.

Instead of berating me, she asks, "Who else used it?"

"Do I dare even say her name?" This comment is the opposite of senseless.

A foghorn from the fishing boats trumpets in the now still air.

"How did you sleep at the inn knowing that in the next room, there lies a dragoness you maimed? Permanently. Giddrath said herself that having tusks is one of the factors that makes you a Giddrathian dragon. And you still took them from her and nearly killed her. S-she was your own historian. She worked with you to support my society." My heart thuds, painfully reminding me of the tormenting drumbeats. "You didn't even blink an eye."

She collects herself. "A traditional execution for crimes against the kingdom includes the removal of tusks from a Giddrathian and said tusks to be shot in the weakest point of a Giddrathian. I have performed such acts before against the vilest of criminals. Murderers, violators, enemy spies."

"She is not any of those things. She was helping us. How do you think she feels, having to work with you? I've seen some violence in my world, even done to me, but I've never seen such callousness done to another living creation before." I shake my head in dismay and turn away from her completely.

"I've had to work with enemies before. I'm sort of doing it right now."

I whirl around. "This is what I'm talking about!" My raised voice wakes up the birds in the canopies. Several squawk and flap away into the night. "Do you not see how even though you would rather not work with us, you have to face the fact that your actions have rippling consequences on the group? She has night terrors, you know that?"

Her tail waves through the sand. "I'd never admit to you that I didn't want to hurt her."

"You recognized her, and you still did. I may work with you for the bettering of the world as we know it, but we are not allies. If I had the choice, I'd stay far from you."

"The same goes for me. Everything is not so simple."

"Oho, why is that, I ask?"

She breathes deeply, placing a claw on her heart, if it even exists. "My daughter's name is Woodlund."

"What?" Immediately, I stand, widen my wings, and snarl, "You … Y-you did that to your own *daughter*?"

"Hold on, hold on–"

"You monster, I feel sick!"

"It's not so simple."

"I'm going back and telling Sparik and everyone." Who else would I tell? What other threat could I throw at her? I cannot defeat her in a war of physical strength but perhaps in one of morals.

"WAIT."

"WHAT?"

"Listen to me. I have a reason for why I was so heartless."

I pause, summon my hate, my anger at the world, at myself, and am about to set it loose.

The dangerous Giddrathian shifts toward me, translucent tears streaming down her cheeks, fleeing her shrunken heart. "Five years ago during the ambush on Capitole, led by Woodlund's sister Eirwen, my soldiers told me what happened to them. What was left amongst the carnage on the battleground was … Woodlund's body. In those stocks, that wasn't Woodlund. Even though it looks just like her, I know my child. The freckles on her cheek, the curl of her horns." From her breast pocket, she takes her leather wallet and gingerly places a picture of a younger her and two dragonesses, smiling in front of the sentient throne. One of them is, in fact, Woodlund, her turquoise eyes alight with wonder and pride. She is carrying the map in her talons. "The dragoness in your room is not my daughter."

Epilogue

STRATUS

I poke the side of my cabbage and potato roll while soft lyre music drifts from the radio above. Why use silverware when I have perfectly nice talons to impale this thing, or perhaps portion it so my eating experience is improved? Dust Devil has his method figured out. He chooses to dip his claws in a bowl of water to cleanse them and *then* cut his ostentatiously presented slice of meat pie. Which cook honestly needs to drizzle that sauce in such a braggy manner?

"Put the sauce on the side," I think. "Not that difficult."

I believe this is the third time Hurricane's brother has ever come to a family dinner in the castle, but he's getting the hang of it. After many days of me bringing leftovers from the kitchen to his room, he's ready to be more social with his family and me.

"I have an idea. I can get some inspiration from the brewers here to bring back when I begin my internship," he said one day while playing a game of croquet.

"That could be cool." I nudged the ball with my wooden mallet to roll through the arch. "When we find Hurricane, we can see what happens."

"Everywhere we've tried is a dead end," Dust Devil said, frustrated. He frapped the ball, missed completely, and had it fly straight into a large shrubbery across the garden. "We should probably play a different game. How about bocce next?"

We flew over to the shapely bush and fished inside the leaves for the camouflaged green ball.

"You make a fair point. Who would we ask next?" I asked. Glancing over to find the landscaper coming over, I nudged him to let the worker be.

"The main wyverness at the concubine we visited a couple weeks ago tried to usher us out. That could've been because of privacy," he said. We sat on the manicured lawn and stared up at the blazing sun. Not a cloud was in the sky. "Hmm. Should I tell my mother?"

"I'd not want her to worry more than she already is. But … I can't *not* imagine her thinking about her own daughter less than we are. Maybe it's time we go talk to her."

He nodded. "Hey, what about your mother? Have you heard from her?"

The birds chirped in the pale-branched trees. I tried to think of something. "Oh, she sent a letter a week ago. 'Hello, how are you? Bring back some designer handbags while you're there!'"

"That's … something, I guess."

I shrugged. "Yeah." *At least my parents talk to me.*

Well, Teal had talked to Dust Devil. Multiple times. I never barged in on their conversations, but he would always leave the bedroom with a tear in his eye and a soft smile. She would come out after with more wrinkles around her eyes than before. They appeared stronger when she grinned after him. Now, the meal sits sadly on my dinner plate, the gold on the porcelain's rim glimmering like a silver lining. I hope I'm interpreting the symbolism of the light correctly, or else he and I have a tough path ahead.

"Stratus, how was bocce ball today?" Cyclone asks from across the dining room table. He sips on lukewarm rosewater soup. I'm sure that flavor is all that his body can take, but the color in his scales is slowly returning.

"The weather moved in quickly." I gesture to the storm pelting rain on the wide, stained-glass windows. Every time lightning flashes, a white, ethereal glow bathes our food. "I'm glad we got at least a game in."

"Who won?"

"Ahem." I place my claws folded together on the table. "Well, actually, Dust Devil did." *I'm taking the chance to stand up for him.* He shifts in his seat, the pillow moving from under him to out in the open.

Cyclone glances up from his meal and looks him up and down. "Hm." That's the most sound that's left his mouth in response to Dust Devil ever since Hurricane left.

"I'm proud of you," Teal says, delicately munching her saffron cornbread. "Bocce is a hard game for some wyverns, even for me when I first played."

"When'd you play *bocce*?" Cyclone asks, narrowing his eyes.

"Oh, a long time ago." She flits her eyes from her husband's face to her food.

The thunder rumbles right outside the window and sends shudders down the polished wood table. My food falls off my talon and onto the floor. Servants waiting by the windows run over and remove the accidental litter. They resume their positions, lurking like gargoyles.

"I'm surprised they didn't perform any live music. Only this radio," Cyclone muses. "They could provide all these super fancy meals over the weeks, but no violin? No harp? Stratus, you play the lyre, right?"

I must have missed fifteen lessons by now. "Yes."

"I remember when you taught Hurricane a couple of songs when you were only ten," Teal says, beaming. "How adorable. Oh, and how incredible you two are still friends to this day." She catches herself and frowns into her food.

We all frown into our food.

"What if we visit her?" Dust Devil suggests.

"No, she's busy," his father says, shaking his head. "That's why she's taking so long. They must be extending her training. We shouldn't bother her while she's working for Windshift. He's giving us sanctuary after all."

Dust Devil scrunches up his snout. *What is he going to say?* "I disagree."

Teal and I side-eye each other.

Cyclone rests his spoon and looks up. "What'd you say?"

"She said she'd be back in a few weeks," he says. "Now the 'few weeks' are becoming a month, and we haven't heard a word. What if something's wrong? We should try to help her."

"No, we're not going to. My word is final," he says. The stress put onto his voice makes him cough into his soup.

His nurse rushes toward and tends to him. Teal rests her head into her claws.

"I'm really concerned about her, Father. She's my sister, for Windshift's sake."

Cyclone straightens his posture while the nurse rubs ointment on his upper neck. "First of all, don't use his name in vain. Second of all, what makes you think you can understand sisterhood?" *Did he accidentally validate Dust Devil there?*

"That has nothing to do with her safety," he says, rolling his eyes.

"Safety? Psh. When was that ever a question in someone's mind?"

"It is in mine."

"If it is in yours, we should test its validity, hm?"

Dust Devil's eyes grow angry, and they argue back and forth over the table. The storm still grumbles outside. His mother casts her gaze around the painted, iridescent walls and flickering, decorative candlelight. Even though she fidgets as if not wanting to be here (who would?), her woeful poise shows how well her scales match the walls.

The radio changes after the serenade of the last harp chord to a faint, utterly unknown line of words. Sharp. Staccato. This is the first time I have to use the word *foreign* to describe this language.

"Why can't you listen to me, Father?" Dust Devil asks desperately. "This is the first conversation we've had in weeks. Why did it have to be like this?"

"What do you have to say that I should listen to? You stole from your mother. And for the most selfish reason I could think of."

"Everyone, *quiet*!" Teal shrieks.

We sit still.

"Stop yelling at each other and listen to the radio," she says. "Now."

We sit silently.

The voice over the soundwaves now is patriotic, masculine, and grave.

"Do you even know what they're saying?" Cyclone asks.

"It sounds like Petrichorish. Only a little," Teal says. "I can sort of make out the words."

Amongst the words I can understand, the most interesting ones ringing above us are as follows: trusted, resurrected, betrayed, dead. *What sort of magic is this? Who's speaking?*

"I can too. Not well." Dust Devil beckons one of the servants to adjust the radio signal. The volume is a tad louder now, which doesn't help much with comprehension.

The radio chops up the sentences like a chef in the kitchen. We hear something we'd never expect.

"Female accomplice, Perra Hurri–" And the radio turns to static as the thunder and lightning bellow and roar outside. The electricity completely goes out, and the servants scurry to find the light box. They bark orders at each other, while we remain silent.

The unextinguished candlelight illuminates our shocked faces. Even Cyclone's anger has subsided. Teal gets up to pace back and forth.

Do they really mean Perra Hurri*cane*? I can't think of anyone else with that name. Plus, why would someone speaking a strange language use a Petrichorish honorific?

There is no doubt about it: Perra Hurricane of Incus has made the news.

She and I joked about cameoing on campus radio for something silly like vandalizing a professor's office, but national news?

Betrayed?

Death?

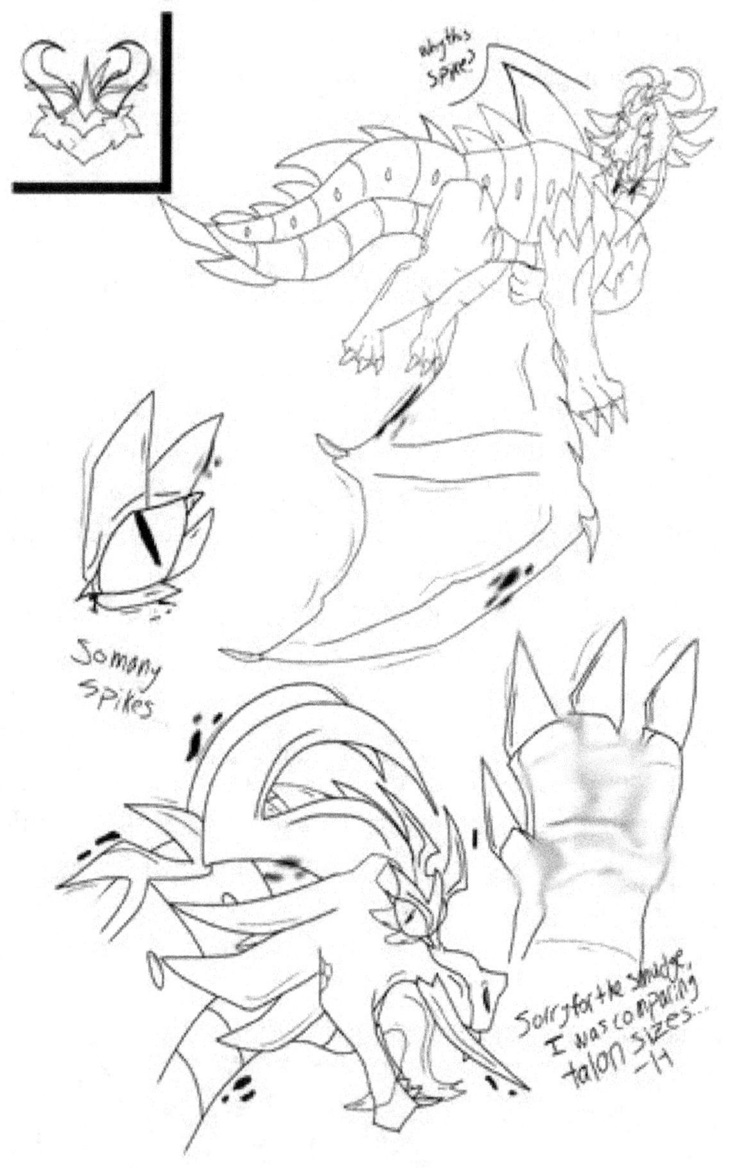

why this spike?
So many spikes
Sorry for the smudge,
I was comparing
talon sizes... -H

ACKNOWLEDGMENTS

Thank you so much for reading *Alpi*! We have two more books to go in the series!

Firstly, this is a genuine thank you to my critics. After reading comments on the pacing and length of my previous books, I have doubled the word count of the other editions to have Book 3 be the longest in the series (~40k words). I had so much fun with giving myself room to write freely and add more scenes to the story. I hope the pacing is much better, and I thank you again for helping me improve my skills!

My gratitude also goes to my friends, whether from my hometown or from college. They have been lovely supporters from day one. A special thank you is given to Clara and Lena, who both leapt to support me even after knowing me for such a short time. Their insightful advice and kindness make me glad to know both women.

I will tip my hat every time to my publisher and editor Jody Dyer, who has looked over my work for two years (wow!) Also, a huge thank you to McKinley Frees who helped Jody polish *Alpi* for it to be the best it can be. Cheers!

Thank you to BoBooks for bringing my designs to life in your beautiful cover art. Your abilities continue to enhance my stories.

Again, I will never stop thanking my Mom and Dad for giving me every opportunity to pursue my dreams in education and writing. I wouldn't be here without them.

Hurricane, Sparik, and Woodlund's journey is not over yet. If you liked this book, please write a review and tell me your thoughts on Amazon and Goodreads! See you next time!

ABOUT THE AUTHOR

Whether in her state of Tennessee or traveling around the world, C.E. Wright wants one thing out of life: joy. So, she pursues it, namely through creativity. Her inspiration comes to her during long walks on the beaches of Amelia Island and relaxing with a warm cup of tea. She started writing her magic at a young age and plans to never stop. When not at her university studying English, creative writing, and languages, she plays classical piano and hones her artistic skills.

Book 1 - Petrichor
Book 2 – Kalder
Book 3 - Alpi

Coming soon ...
Book 4 - Ióda
Book 5 - Maelstrom

Follow C.E. Wright here:
Instagram: c_e_wright
Twitter: @ce_wright8
Tumblr, ArtFight: c-e-wright
Facebook: CE Wright